HOUSE OF SECRETS

Books by Beverly Lewis

GIRLS ONLY (GO!)
Youth Fiction

Dreams on Ice	Follow the Dream
Only the Best	Better Than Best
A Perfect Match	Photo Perfect
Reach for the Stars	Star Status

SUMMERHILL SECRETS
Youth Fiction

Whispers Down the Lane	House of Secrets
Secret in the Willows	Echoes in the Wind
Catch a Falling Star	Hide Behind the Moon
Night of the Fireflies	Windows on the Hill
A Cry in the Dark	Shadows Beyond the Gate

HOLLY'S HEART
Youth Fiction

Best Friend, Worst Enemy	Straight-A Teacher
Secret Summer Dreams	No Guys Pact
Sealed With a Kiss	Little White Lies
The Trouble With Weddings	Freshman Frenzy
California Crazy	Mystery Letters
Second-Best Friend	Eight Is Enough
Good-Bye, Dressel Hills	It's a Girl Thing

www.BeverlyLewis.com

SummerHill Secrets

HOUSE OF SECRETS

Beverly Lewis

BETHANY HOUSE PUBLISHERS
MINNEAPOLIS, MINNESOTA 55438

Published by Bethany House Publishers
11400 Hampshire Avenue South
Bloomington, Minnesota 55438
www.bethanyhouse.com

Bethany House Publishers is a Division of
Baker Book House Company, Grand Rapids, Michigan.

Printed in the United States of America

Library of Congress Cataloging-in-Publication Data

Lewis, Beverly, 1949–
   House of secrets / Beverly Lewis.
      p. cm. — (SummerHill secrets ; 6)
   Summary: Merry asks God to help her find her friend's missing mother.
   ISBN 1-55661-872-7 (pbk.)
   [1. Christian life—Fiction. 2. Friendship—Fiction. 3. Mystery and detective stories.] I. Title. II. Series: Lewis, Beverly, 1949– SummerHill secrets ; 6.
PZ7.L58464Hq   1996
[Fic]—dc20   96–25298
                                                   CIP
                                                     AC

To
Verna Flower,
whose loving hospitality
eased my homesickness
during college days . . .
and
who read
my first book manuscript
with editorial encouragement.
Thanks, Aunt Verna,
for your prayers
and love
all these years.

BEVERLY LEWIS is a speaker, teacher, and the best-selling author of the HOLLY'S HEART series. She has written more than thirty books for teens and children. Many of her articles and stories have appeared in the nation's top magazines.

Beverly is a member of The National League of American Pen Women, the Society of Children's Book Writers and Illustrators, and Colorado Christian Communicators. She and her husband, Dave, along with their three teenagers, live in Colorado. She fondly remembers their cockapoo named Cuddles, who used to snore to Mozart!

You spread out our sins before you
—our secret sins—and see them all.

—Psalm 90:8 TLB

ONE

Eerie and still, the study hall classroom echoed my words. "What do you mean your mom's disappeared?"

I stared at my friend Chelsea Davis. Her thick auburn hair fell forward on one shoulder.

Her voice trembled as she searched in her schoolbag. "Sometime in the night . . . she . . . Mom must've written this note. And now . . ." Chelsea paused, staring at the folded paper in her hand. "Now she's gone."

She scanned the study hall cautiously, waiting until the last student vacated the room. Then she handed me the note.

"Do you really want me to read this?" I said, noticing how very pale her face had become.

Chelsea nodded, and slowly, I unfolded the paper.

Before you wake up, I'll be gone. Don't try to find me. I'm happy where I'll be.

My throat felt tight as I read the frightful words. Startled, I refolded the note.

I'm happy where I'll be. . . . Questions nagged at me, but I said nothing.

Chelsea's voice cracked, breaking the silence. "I guess you never know how important your family is until one of them is gone."

Her words struck a chord. I, too, had experienced the loss of a family member. My twin sister, Faithie, had died of leukemia at age seven.

But this? This was far different. Surely Mrs. Davis would return to her family. Maybe she and Mr. Davis had argued; maybe she needed space—time to sort things out.

"Give it a few days," I said almost without thinking. "Surely your mom'll come back home."

Chelsea sighed. "I hope you're right, but this morning I poked around in Mom's closet. She didn't take much with her, but she's definitely gone." Chelsea stared at the underside of her watch. "For no reason, she just walked out . . . left us. Dad and me."

I slipped my assignment notebook into my schoolbag. "How's your dad handling things?"

"Well, we talked at breakfast." She had a faraway look in her eyes. "You see, Mom had these new friends . . . a super-weird guy and his wife. They were always whispering with my mom the few times they came to our house. They were into some of the same stuff Mom likes—astrological charts, seances, and stuff like that. Anyway, Mom went with them for coffee several times about a month ago, around the time she got laid off from work. Next thing I knew, she was going to their house for supper, and a couple of times the three of them went to some metaphysical fair in Philadelphia."

"Did they invite your dad along?"

Chelsea nodded. "Mom and Dad both went to a secret meeting with them at a hotel once." A frown crept between her eyes. "The thing is, Mom seemed awfully excited about these people—about their mysterious activities."

"What about the meeting? What was *that* all about?"

"Beats me, but after the first time, Dad refused to go again. Mom was furious. I heard them talking in the kitchen late one night, and I crawled out of bed to listen at the top of the steps. Mom was beside herself—nearly hysterical—trying to get Dad to see what she said was 'the true light.' Over and over she kept saying it—that he was resisting 'the true light.' "

Describing the scene really seemed to bug my friend—the crimped sound in her usually mellow voice and the way she blinked back angry tears told me more than her words. Somewhere along the line, Chelsea Davis had declared herself an atheist. I wondered if she resented her mom for this spiritual encounter—or whatever was going on.

I took a deep breath. "Do you think your mom's friends influenced her to leave?"

Chelsea shook her head. "All I know is that Mom seemed desperate to make some sort of pledge or oath, but she couldn't get Dad interested. From what I overheard, he thought the whole thing was ridiculous."

"An oath? What for?"

"I don't know exactly," she replied. "Mom wanted to keep attending the meetings. She pleaded with Dad, trying to persuade him, but he wouldn't go back."

"Did your mom ever go again?" I asked, wondering

what on earth had really happened with Chelsea's mother.

"Three or four more times, I think. In fact, Mom was hardly home all last week. Oh, and something else . . ."

I cringed. There was more?

"She suddenly started cooking up these vegetarian meals for us—wouldn't allow red meat or pork in the house. And she refused to drink water or anything else with her meal. Crazy stuff like that."

This was beginning to sound truly strange. Scary too.

"But the weirdest thing about it—Mom seemed super relaxed. Content, I guess you'd say," Chelsea added. "And she'd been horribly miserable before and depressed about losing her position at the hospital."

I'd heard about the cutback. "Too bad her job was phased out. Your mom loved her work."

"The hospital only needs so many administrative nurses, and she had worked there the fewest years." Chelsea puffed out her cheeks, then forced the air out. "Then these people, this couple, seemed to appear out of nowhere."

"What do you think they wanted—I mean, isn't it a little bizarre?"

Chelsea gathered up her books, and we headed for the hallway. "I wish I knew."

My heart went out to my friend. "I'll do whatever I can to help you," I volunteered, keeping pace with her.

"Thanks." She gave me a pained smile. "And, uh, Merry, if you don't mind, could you keep it quiet—you know, all the stuff I told you?"

"Count on me," I reassured her.

We walked down the hushed hallway to the long row of lockers. It was late. We'd missed the school bus, yet Chelsea took her time opening her combination lock, and I found myself deep in thought as I did the same. *How would I feel if* my *mom vanished into thin air?*

We dropped off our books and sorted out only what we needed for homework. I cast a rueful glance at my friend several lockers away. Chelsea had just confided a truly deep secret, not knowing I'd been praying for her all through middle school and now as a freshman in high school. Sometimes she put up with my talk about God—the God she said didn't exist. Most of the time, she wasn't interested.

But what Chelsea said next really rattled me. Shook me straight to my heart.

"I'm . . . I'm scared, Mer," she cried, standing in front of her locker. "I'm afraid I'll never see my mom again!"

I ran to her and let her bury her face in the shoulder of my jacket. "Oh, Chelsea, you will. You will." I hoped it was true.

She clung to me, her body heaving with sobs. "I have to find her . . . I want her back," her muffled voice said into my shoulder.

I could almost feel the autumn chill, the cold, damp rawness, seeping through the cracks in the windowpanes as Chelsea cried.

Silently, I prayed.

TWO

After Chelsea dried her eyes, I hurried to use the pay phone inside the school's main doors.

Mom answered on the first ring. "Where *are* you, Merry?"

"Still at school, but don't worry. Something came up. Could you come get me? Chelsea too?"

"I'll leave right now," she said without probing.

It would take Mom about fifteen minutes to arrive. We lived in a remote Amish farm community on the outskirts of Lancaster County. We weren't plain folk or farmers, but most of our neighbors were. SummerHill Lane was actually a long dirt road that wound its way past fertile fields and pastureland owned by Old Order Amish. I must admit, it wasn't easy leaving the picturesque setting behind every morning, even to come to school.

Chelsea and I decided to wait inside the school's double doors, peering out through the window every now and then. To pass the time, we read our boring English assignments out loud. It was Chelsea's idea. "This way, we can knock down some homework before we ever get home," she said.

Soon, my mom pulled up to the curb, and we hurried out to meet her. Chelsea sat in the backseat; I in front.

"Something came up and we missed the bus," I offered as an explanation.

"Nothing academic, I hope." Mom's eyebrows flew up.

"Oh no, nothing like that." I was quick to set her scholastic worries at ease.

Off we sped toward the highway. Chelsea blew her nose. I hoped she wasn't crying again, but I didn't turn around to investigate.

"Everything okay?" Mom asked, glancing in her rearview mirror. She was like that—picked right up on things.

I'd promised to keep Chelsea's secret, so I ignored Mom's question. "What a hectic day. And the homework! I think the teachers have totally spaced out what it's like being fourteen. You'd think they'd try to ease their youngest students into the halls of higher learning. Instead, I think they have a contest going to see who can pile on the most assignments." I groaned for emphasis.

Mom smiled dutifully. "Speaking of higher learning, your brother called today over the noon hour. He sounded homesick, says dorm life is dismal."

I tried not to snicker. *Silly Skip. Probably misses good home cooking and his own bed.* He'd made such a pompous fuss about going off to college—managed to get top grades his senior year—and couldn't wait to show the world what a cool college man he was. Now he was coming home for the weekend—homesick! It was hard to believe my haughty big brother had actually admitted his weakness to Mom.

I flashed a superior grin. "Is this the same smart aleck we sent off to college at the end of August?"

"Now, Merry, you have no idea what you're talking about," Mom defended. "Skip simply wants to come home for the weekend. I think it's wonderful."

She would think that. Six weeks into the first semester, and he already needed a steak-and-potato fix. Truly disappointing to say the least. I just hoped Skip wouldn't make a habit of returning often. I'd waited a long time to have the run of the house—and all the parental attention.

Suddenly, my thoughts turned back to Chelsea. Here I was fretting over having to share my parents' affections, and her mom wasn't even around anymore. Overwhelming feelings weighed on me—worry and concern for my friend. What would Chelsea do?

Mom turned into the driveway in front of Chelsea's house, an old, two-story Colonial similar to ours.

"Call me," I said as Chelsea slid out and closed the car door.

"I will, and thanks for the ride, Mrs. Hanson. 'Bye, Merry," she called.

A lump rose in my throat as I watched my friend lean into the wind, heading up the brick walkway toward the house. *Please help her, Lord*, I prayed.

I pulled my jacket tightly against me and longed to curl up in front of a crackling fire somewhere, but not because I was cold. I was terrified.

Slowly, Mom backed out of the driveway and headed down the hill. I stared out the window at high, wispy clouds moving rapidly across a hazy October sky. Indian summer days were fast spinning into deep autumn. Flaming leaves of orange, red, and shimmering gold danced on thick, wide branches on either side of SummerHill Lane.

How could a mother abandon her family and her home at such an incredible time? How, at anytime? I thought of Mrs. Davis tending her beloved flower beds, now ready to be spaded under for the winter. And her tinkling wind chimes, dozens of them, lovingly crafted by her own hands. How could she leave it all behind?

Most of all, how could she leave her husband, a charming, jovial man of forty-two with no sign of balding and apparently no hint of a midlife crisis? And Chelsea, too, their only child?

A horse and buggy caught my attention as it *clip-clopped* and swayed up the hill toward us. I waved, recognizing our Amish friends in the front of the gray box-shaped buggy typical of the Lancaster County Old Order. "Look, it's Rachel Zook and her mother," I said, noting their matching woolen shawls and black bonnets.

Mom let the buggy pass before making the left-hand turn into our gravel driveway. "Must be headed for a quilting frolic," she observed. "Their potatoes are harvested by now, and most all the corn is cut and shocked, so it's time for visiting and quilting. Amish women live for such things, you know."

I sighed. "I wonder how Rachel likes going to frolics with her mother instead of school."

"She's following in her ancestors' footsteps," Mom said. "How would *you* feel quitting school after only eight grades?"

"I'd miss it. Especially my friends," I said, thinking of

Lissa, Chelsea . . . and Jonathan Klein.

"I suppose Rachel will be baptized into the Amish church next summer," Mom said.

"That's what she says. Rachel wants to get married and have lots of babies." I didn't tell Mom that one of the Yoder boys down the lane had taken Rachel to a Sunday Singing recently. Not even her own parents were aware of it. Serious Amish courting took place under the covering of night—the way Rachel's people had been courting for three hundred years.

Mom glanced at me. "Have you heard from Levi lately?"

"Not for several weeks." Levi Zook, Rachel's older brother, had gone off to a Mennonite college in Virginia, turning his back on his Amish upbringing. Levi and I and all the Zook children had grown up together. Our properties shared the same boundary—a thick grove of willow trees. Levi and I had promised to write to each other this school year.

My parents hadn't been especially thrilled about the idea of Levi and me becoming close friends. I should say *Mom* wasn't too keen on it. Dad, however, was more easygoing. He'd even made attempts to get better acquainted with Levi on several occasions.

"Life is much different now for Levi Zook, I would guess. He's probably busy with his studies," Mom said, attempting to make me feel better.

Truth was, Levi hadn't thought it fair to tie me down while he was off at Bible school. Besides, we'd made no romantic promises to each other. He was free to meet other girls. I, however, had my heart set on Jon Klein, a boy in our youth group at church—also a freshman at James Buchanan High.

Jon was a wordplay freak. I liked to refer to him as the Alliteration Wizard. Unfortunately for him, I was gaining ground—soon to topple his status. The two of us had become so consistently clever at conversing using only similar beginning consonant sounds that I'd begun to talk alliteration-eze almost automatically. Especially at home.

Today, though, a cloud of gloom hung over me. Chelsea's mom was in trouble, and my friend had asked me not to tell anyone. The secret burden was horribly heavy.

I looked back up at the sky. The fast-moving, high clouds were a sure sign of a storm. Trees swayed back and forth in their dazzling costumes. There was so much Chelsea's mom would miss if she stayed away: The deep orange of the Pennsylvania harvest moon, crisp morning walks, birds flying south for the winter . . . Thanksgiving Day, Christmas . . .

I shivered, thinking of Chelsea living out the lonely days or months ahead. There had to be something I could do.

A small-scale investigation might turn up some leads. That's what Chelsea needed: Someone to help her poke around a bit. Someone to help her solve the heartbreaking mystery.

I couldn't wait to phone her.

THREE

Running toward my house, I darted in through the back door, eager to use the phone. I nearly stumbled over my cats—Shadrach, Meshach, and Abednego—and one ivory kitten named Lily White, bright as a lily.

All four cats were lined up comically beside two empty bowls near the back door—my cue.

"Oh, I'm sorry." I squatted down beside the foursome. "You're waiting for snack time, aren't you, babies? You know I'd never forget you guys on purpose, don'tcha?" I marched to the fridge. "It's just that I got stuck at school. That's why there's no milky-moo."

Mom joined me inside, car keys jangling. "Oops, guess I overlooked something." She smiled knowingly, spying the hungry anticipation on the furry faces.

"It's not your fault, Mom," I said. "I'm the one who missed the bus, remember?"

We laughed about how spoiled the cats had become. "Thanks to their doting mama," chortled Mom.

It was true. I *had* spoiled my cats rotten. But wasn't it the sensible, loving thing to do with felines so fine? Programming them to expect fresh, rich cow's milk every day after school was part of being a pampering pet owner. Or as Mom said, a doting mama.

"You'll have to forgive me this time," I said, pouring the raw, cream-rich milk into two medium-sized bowls. Abednego, being the oldest and fattest, had his own opinion about pecking order. He allowed only his next-in-line brother, Shadrach, to share his bowl.

I grinned and brushed my hand over their backs. "Mama's so sorry about the late snack."

Sitting there on the floor hearing the gentle lapping sounds of healthy, contented cats, I thought again of my friend Chelsea. She needed a phone call. Now.

Without another word to my furry friends, I scanned our country kitchen. Mom had evidently gone upstairs.

Quickly, I crossed the room to the phone, picked it up, and listened for the dial tone. I knew Chelsea might not be able to talk openly if her dad was within earshot, but at least she could hear me out.

"Hi, Chels," I said when she answered. "It's Merry and I've got a genius idea."

"You say that about all your ideas." She wasn't laughing.

I was smart enough to know it wasn't a compliment. "Can you talk now?" I asked.

"I'm talking, aren't I?" She sounded depressed.

"But is your dad around?"

"Daddy's still at work. Someone has to work around here."

"Yeah."

"So what is it—your genius plan?" she asked.

"Well, I've been thinking. We oughta go over your

place with a fine-tooth comb. You know, search for clues."

"I thought of that, too." Her voice sounded small. "Do you wanna come over?"

"Sure."

"Tomorrow after school?"

"Okay, good. Have you heard anything more about your mom?" As soon as I voiced the words, I wished I'd kept quiet.

"No, but there was an urgent message from the bank on Dad's computer when I got home," she said. "It seems that some money is missing from my parents' joint account." Her voice was hollow.

"You're kidding?"

"Not one word to anyone, you hear?" She was silent. Then—"I can't believe Mom would do this. She'd *never* do anything like this if . . ." Chelsea stopped, and I heard her breath coming into the phone in short little puffs.

"It's okay, Chels," I said. "You can trust me."

"Oh, I don't know. I keep wondering if someone's brainwashed Mom—taken control of her somehow. Have you ever read about stuff like that?"

"Brainwashed? Why do you think that?"

Chelsea whimpered into the phone. "I have a weird feeling about that guy and his wife."

"Any idea who they are?"

She exhaled. "Maybe Dad remembers their names. I sure don't."

"Why don't you ask him when he gets home?" It was just a suggestion. We didn't have much else to go on.

"I'll wait and see how he feels tonight."

I wanted so badly to tell her not to worry, that I was trusting God to work things out. But that was just the sort of talk that often disconnected Chelsea from me. So I said, "Hey, call me anytime, okay? Even in the middle of the night if you want. I'll put Skip's portable phone in my bedroom, and no one'll ever know the difference."

"Won't the ringing wake up your parents?" she asked.

"Dad's working the late shift at the hospital, so he won't be here tonight, and Mom's a heavy sleeper. She'll never hear it."

"And you *will?*"

I chuckled. "I'll stick the phone under my pillow if that makes you feel better."

"It's a deal." Her voice was stronger. "Well, I've gotta figure out something for supper. Dad likes big meals."

I remembered that Chelsea had said they'd been enduring all-vegetarian meals for the past week. "Surprise your dad and make something gourmet," I suggested.

"Yeah, right. I'll talk to you tomorrow, if not before."

"Okay. Good-bye." I hung up the phone, concerned about the latest information. The message about the bank business didn't sound good. Could someone actually be coerced to pull money out of their bank account?

When Mom came downstairs, I wanted to ask her about it, but I'd promised not to tell anyone. So I held it all in—every single heart-wrenching detail.

FOUR

"When's Skip coming home?" I asked Mom.

She straightened up from putting a frozen casserole in the oven. "He should arrive by suppertime tomorrow."

"So . . . he's really homesick, huh?" I hoped Mom would give some other reason for his coming to spend the weekend. I was downright worried he might move back.

"Adjusting to college life is harder for some students than others," she explained. "I think Skip may be having a little difficulty. Sometimes I wish we'd found a Christian college for him to attend."

I reached for two dinner plates; it was going to be just Mom and me tonight. "Well, *I* sure don't want to go off to some heathen college campus."

Mom scowled. "Your brother is *not* attending a heathen college. There are several wonderful Christian organizations right there on campus. In fact, one group meets in Skip's science lab after hours. He said something about being invited to one of the meetings last week."

"Oh." That's all I said. There was no arguing with Mom.

Later that night while working through a pile of

homework, I found a slip of paper wedged down in one of the pockets of my three-ring binder. I pulled it out.

A photography contest notice! How could I have overlooked this? My heart leaped up as I thought about the annual event. As a ninth-grade freshman, I would have oodles of opportunities to display my talents at Buchanan High School, starting this year! The competition would be stiff, but I could hardly wait.

One of my passions in life was photography, followed by a close second—poetry. Especially romantic sonnets. Not writing them but *reading* them, and occasionally agonizing over the poetry. And if I were completely open about my hobbies, I'd also admit that I loved word games—and Jon Klein included . . . probably.

Jon hadn't yet reached the level of maturity required to acknowledge such profound things as love. *Give him another year*, I figured. *Maybe then he'll start seeing me for what I am. Girlfriend material.*

The biggest roadblock was our new pastor's daughter. Ashley Horton was the kind of girl people—especially guys—noticed when she walked into a room.

Ashley wasn't beautiful only on the outside; she did have some depth of soul. She was kind to animals and never spoke out of turn in Sunday school class. Ashley wasn't a typical PK (Preacher's Kid), and people knew it the first time they met her. She didn't seem interested in pushing the limits like some ministers' daughters. In other words, she wasn't wild. She was genuinely nice. A little dense, but nice.

One other thing: Ashley had developed a huge crush on Jon. Just plain couldn't keep her eyes off him. And everyone knew it. Everyone except Jon.

It started to rain. In spite of intermittent lightning flashes, I settled into working two pages of algebra, sailing right through—thanks to getting help from Dad early in the school year. Everything about solving unknown factors made complete sense to me now. If only there was a way to solve the unknowns in Chelsea's life.

Where *could* her mom have gone? And why?

Questions haunted me all evening. By the time I finished my homework, the phone was ringing. I scooted my desk chair back and hurried to stand in the doorway, listening.

Mom's voice floated upstairs. Ashley Horton was on the line. "Take the call in Skip's room if you'd like," she suggested.

I hurried down the hall to my brother's vacant bedroom. "Hello?" I said as I picked up the portable phone and sat on his bed.

"Hi, Merry. I was wondering about that photography contest at school. I suppose you're going to enter." It was almost a question, but not quite.

"Well, yes. I plan to."

"I thought maybe you could give me some ideas for subject matter—you know, the types of scenery or things that took first place other years."

Was this girl for real?

"Well, I suppose there are lots of things you could do," I said, trying not to patronize or give away any of my own genius ideas.

"Could you give me some examples of shots that *might* be winning photos?" she asked.

"Oh, sure . . . things like windmills and Amish settings. White dairy barns might be a good choice or rustic tobacco sheds. Let your imagination go. But watch your lighting, depth perception, things like that."

"Oh, Merry, those are such good ideas!" she gushed. "Thank you so much."

"It was nothing." Then remembering about an important taboo, I warned, "Be careful around the Amish. They don't want to be photographed, so I wouldn't advise flaunting a camera in front of them."

"Aw, but they're so adorable in those cute long dresses and aprons. Those black felt hats the men wear . . . and their long beards."

Oh, please, I thought. *I don't believe this!*

"Whatever you do, Ashley, if you care anything about the Amish people, you won't sneak shots of them."

"So you really think taking pictures of plain people is a problem?" She sounded as if she was speaking alliteration-eze, the word game Jon and I played.

I wanted to make her promise not to offend the Amish that way. "Please, just don't do it, Ashley. I'm serious."

That seemed to subdue her. "All right," she said. "If you're sure about this . . . but I guess I just don't understand."

Ashley and her family had moved here last year from somewhere north of Denver, Colorado. Naturally, they wouldn't know much about Amish tradition.

I explained. "If you want to know the reason why they don't approve of having their pictures taken, read the Ten Commandments—Exodus twenty, verse four. They take the verse literally. We'll talk tomorrow at school."

"Okay. And thanks again very much. You've been a big help."

"See ya." I hung up.

I could just imagine Ashley rushing off to her father's study at their parsonage to look up the Bible verse this very instant. That was Ashley.

I hoped I'd convinced her to keep her camera lens away from the Amish. It's strange how people often want to do the very thing they're told *not* to do. Must be human nature.

Anyway, as I headed back to my own room, I decided to make a list of my top-five favorite picture-taking scenes in SummerHill by tomorrow.

Tomorrow . . .

Chelsea and I would search for clues at her house tomorrow. I hoped that if there were any, they'd lead us to her mother.

And tomorrow evening Skip was coming home.

I hurried downstairs to gather up my brood of cats for the night. Skip despised my pets. "Maybe if they weren't ordinary alley cats, I'd feel differently," he'd told me once.

But I knew better. The real reason he resented my precious, purry critters was his snobbish mentality. Skip wished I'd be more selective about my pets. Stray cats— stray anything—disgusted him. For a person studying to become a medical doctor, his nose-in-the-air approach to life didn't fit. Not in my opinion.

Downstairs, I picked up Lily White and cuddled her as I opened the back door. "Come to beddy-bye, little boys," I called out into the night.

Shadrach and Meshach came running. They were only slightly damp because they'd been hiding in their favorite place—under the gazebo. Abednego, true to form, was missing.

"Where's your big brother?" I asked them.

Meow, meowsy-meow.

"Oh, so you think he's chasing a mouse in the willow grove? Well, we can't wait up for him all night." I headed for the back stairway, hoping Abednego wouldn't come inside all muddy. That wouldn't set well with Mom.

After a warm bath, I snuggled into bed with my Bible and teen devotional. I slid the portable phone under my pillow as promised. Just in case Chelsea called.

Abednego, surprisingly clean, decided to grace us with his presence at last. He took his sweet time getting situated on top of my comforter. Now all four of my cats were safe and snug.

I reread the selection for the day, thinking about the poem that accompanied the devotional prayer. Feeling drowsy, I turned out the light. "Sweet dreams," I whispered into the darkness as the sounds of soft purring mingled with the gentle *tinkle-pat-pat* of rain on the roof.

In the stillness, I prayed—first for Chelsea, then for her mother. "And, Lord," I added a short PS, "will you please help us find something tomorrow that'll point us in the right direction? I'm trusting you. Amen."

To say that I was trusting my heavenly Father was all well and good. Now I had to hang on to those words and live by them. For Chelsea's sake. And mine.

FIVE

The halls of Buchanan High were clogged with students, some trying to get to lockers, others milling around.

Jon Klein seemed unruffled, however, his arms loaded with textbooks and binders for his morning classes. His light brown hair was combed back on the sides, and he was rejoicing at having sneaked up on me. "What's the weird word, Merry?" he babbled.

I chuckled. "Isn't it 'what's the *good* word'?"

"Good won't work with *w* words," he replied, alliterating almost without thinking. That's how it seemed, anyway.

I looked up at him, trying to secure a soon-to-be avalanche of books in my locker. "You know something? I think you're getting too good at this word game of ours."

"Here, help's on high." He reached over my head and grabbed my precarious pile of books off the top shelf with his free hand. "Being barraged by books is . . ." He paused, searching for a *b* word.

"Bad," I said, filling in the blank.

"Boom!"

"Bane," I shot back.

"Barely believable."

The Alliteration Wizard had won again. Or had he? I felt a surge of words coming.

"Being barraged by books is basically a bumpy battle." A triumph for me!

Jon's brown eyes blinked in surprise. "But . . . but . . . bested I be."

"Yes—I won!"

He grinned and nodded. "Not bad for a gir—" He stopped.

"Don't you dare say it!"

"Okay, you win. *This* time."

After I reorganized my books, I grabbed a notebook and was ready for the first bell.

"See ya later," he called, catching up with some guys heading for his homeroom.

" 'Bye." I walked alone to mine, wondering where Chelsea was hiding out. I stopped by her locker and noticed Belita Sanchez, the girl whose locker was next to my friend's. "Have you seen Chelsea today?"

"Maybe she's running late," Belita commented.

"Well, if you see her, please tell Chelsea I'm looking for her. Okay?"

"That's cool." Belita started to turn away, then she reached out to touch my arm. "Merry, is something wrong with Chelsea?" Her dark eyes searched mine.

"What do you mean?"

"Oh, she just seemed tense and really stressed yesterday."

I didn't want to lie. "Chelsea's . . . uh, she's . . ."

Belita raised one eyebrow in a quizzical slant, waiting for my faltering response.

Then—"Hey, Merry!" came a familiar voice.

I turned to see our auburn-haired friend dashing down the hall toward us. Breathing a sigh, I was more than glad to see her. "Oh, good, you're here."

"Dad drove me," she said, indicating with her sea-green eyes that something was up.

"Hi, Belita. How's it going?" she said as I hung around. The girls exchanged small talk, then Chelsea and I hurried off to homeroom just as the first bell rang.

"You look exhausted," I said. "Did you sleep at all?"

"Not much." Her face was sallow and her eyes lacked their usual brightness.

I felt sick with concern. Chelsea seemed even more depressed than yesterday. "More bad news?" I asked.

"Uh-huh. But I can't talk about it until we're absolutely alone. Somewhere private."

I followed her into our homeroom, where Mrs. Fields, who was also our English teacher, greeted us. "Morning, girls." She stood up as we skittered to our desks. "Several of you have been asking about the photography contest."

I leaned forward, listening intently.

Chelsea whispered to me, "You look too eager."

Our mutual friend, Lissa Vyner, two desks away, turned around. "I heard that," she mouthed, then curled her fingers in a delicate wave.

I waved back as the teacher continued. "This contest is one of the most important extracurricular events of the year here at Buchanan High. The judging is strict, and the photography exhibit is always very professional. Last year two students tied for first place initially, but the panel of judges agreed to go back to the table and choose a definite winner."

Amazing! I wondered who'd ended up with the coveted trophy. Quickly, I made a mental note to ask Mrs. Fields after class. I *had* to know.

"For interested students," she continued, "the forms, as well as additional information, will be here on my desk. You may pick them up before leaving for first-period class."

Lissa raised her hand. "What's the deadline for the contest?"

Mrs. Fields glanced at the information sheet. "Here we are. The deadline for all applicants is November fourth." She looked at the wall calendar. "Exactly one month from today."

I wrote the date on my assignment tablet with the words: *Remember to do something truly amazing!*

Mrs. Fields took roll, then the principal's voice came over the intercom. "Good morning, students. Today is Friday, October fourth. We will have schedule A today. Faculty and students, please make a note of this."

I folded my arms and tuned him out. Why did Mr. Eastman recite the same boring things *every* morning? He greeted the student body collectively, said the day, month, and date—and reminded us whether today was a schedule A or B day.

I'm not sure why the monotony of it bothered me so much. Maybe because we were now in high school. Wouldn't it make better sense to encourage students to figure out what the day's schedule was on their own?

Thinking for yourself was part of growing up.

"And now . . . our national anthem," the intercom boomed.

I stood up, joining the other students. The taped rendition warbled in places, and I wondered if it was wearing out—like Mr. Eastman.

Dear old Mr. Eastman . . .

My mom had shown me his yearbook picture from twenty-two years earlier when *she* was in high school. I thought he looked almost elderly back then.

"Mr. Eastman always had a heart for kids," Mom told me when I'd first asked about him. "Times have changed, and he probably should retire. But it's a free country, and the dear old fellow's hanging in there."

"Barely," I said. "You should hear what he does every morning for opening exercises—at least that's what he calls it."

I told her.

Mom smiled in recognition. "That's precisely how he always started the day. Just be thankful he doesn't personally sing 'The Star-Spangled Banner' anymore."

I gasped. "Are you serious?"

"Mr. Eastman warbled it every morning all through my high school years." Mom burst out laughing. "Except when he was ill. Then the secretary would invite the whole school to sing in unison."

"That's incredible. What was his voice like?"

"Oh, your average Joe's—nothing special."

"So it wasn't too obnoxious?" I asked.

"Not really. I think it was simply the idea of having

the principal croon out the national anthem on the PA system."

"The what?"

"The public address system," she explained.

"Oh yeah—back in the *olden* days." I smiled. So did Mom. She was a good sport.

Hearing Mom talk about her high school days and Mr. Eastman made me curious about other things. The age of our school building, for instance. James Buchanan High was a picture postcard building of dark red brick— two stories high—partly covered with ivy. The exterior windows jutted out with white sash bars below. Inside, there were hinged transom windows that actually opened high above each classroom door.

The vine-covered brick structure smelled old, almost musty on rainy days when the windows had to be kept closed. I could see why Mom loved the place. She adored antiques; old buildings included. It was one of the reasons we lived in a drafty hundred-plus-year-old farmhouse. One of the reasons why Mom had furnished our house with beautiful, gleaming heirlooms. Even *my* room, where a massive antique white-pine desk graced one entire wall.

The bell for first period jolted me out of my musing. I hurried to Mrs. Fields's desk and stood in line behind Lissa and two other girls waiting for the information sheets and application forms for the photography contest.

On the way toward the door, I asked Mrs. Fields about last year's winner.

"Oh yes," she said. "It was really quite something.

The winner turned out to be Mr. Eastman's grand-nephew."

"Really? I don't think I know him. Did he graduate last year?" I moved aside to let students pass.

"Why, no, I believe Randall's a junior this year."

Randall Eastman. The name didn't click. Yet I was mighty curious.

"Well, thanks," I said. "I'd really like to meet him."

"He's not much into athletics, as you may guess," Mrs. Fields said. "You can usually find him in the library, in the reference section."

"Okay, thanks." I hurried to catch up with Chelsea and Lissa.

❧   ❧

Later, in algebra, Ashley Horton passed me a note.

Hi, Merry,
I read the fourth commandment last night—the one about not making any graven image. I really want to thank you for pointing this out to me. You can be sure I WON'T be taking pictures of any Amish folk.

—A.H.

I smiled at her across a row of desks, feeling a bit relieved. One less thing to worry about.

Leaning back in my seat, I listened as the teacher introduced the next chapter and took good notes so I'd understand how to do the algebra problems at home. I glanced over at Chelsea. Her eyes were glazed over, and she seemed to be staring into midair.

Oh, Chelsea . . . Chelsea. What horrible things have happened since yesterday? I wondered.

The blood had drained from her face. Even as fair-skinned as she was, it seemed she'd turned a chalky white.

Without warning, she keeled over. Fainted right on the spot!

My heart pounded ninety miles an hour as I leaped out of my seat.

SIX

Kids gasped as Chelsea's limp body slipped off her chair and onto the floor. The teacher asked one of the girls to get the school nurse.

I made a beeline to my friend, knelt down, and checked her breathing and pulse. Reaching for some paper off Chelsea's desk, I began to fan her, pushing the thick covering of hair away from her face. *Dear Lord, please help!*

The nurse arrived almost immediately. I moved back to make room, watching as she placed her hand gently behind Chelsea's neck. She opened a small bottle of spirits of ammonia and waved it under Chelsea's nose.

The harsh, irritating odor did the trick. Chelsea wrinkled her nose, her eyes fluttered, and she sat up.

The smell took my breath away.

"Whoa, smells like week-old underwear," one of the boys said, scrunching up his face.

"Worse!" remarked another, holding his nose.

Guys, I thought. *Will they ever grow up?*

Chelsea sat up and looked around, blinking her long lashes.

"Let's see if you can get up, hon," the nurse said. She and I helped Chelsea stand up. Everyone else went back to their desks, the excitement over.

Chelsea leaned on both the nurse and me as we assisted her out of the room and down the hall.

"You okay?" I asked as we headed toward the nurse's office.

"I don't know what happened," she mumbled. "One minute I was sitting in my seat listening to the algebra assignment, and the next, I was on the floor."

"It's called fainting," I said, hoping to humor her. She still looked ghastly pale.

The nurse's room was a square cubicle where a cot and chair took up most of the space on one wall. A small desk and a second chair filled the opposite side of the room.

Kindly, the nurse got Chelsea settled into the chair. "Now"—she surveyed my friend—"tell me about breakfast. Did you have any?"

Chelsea shook her head.

"Your first mistake." The nurse gave a nervous chuckle.

I could see Chelsea wasn't interested in an interrogation. She stared into space almost defiantly.

"Are you having your period?" the nurse inquired.

"Not quite yet," Chelsea answered.

"Well, you're certainly welcome to lie down and rest here until you feel stronger. Or," she said, glancing at me briefly, "would you rather call your parents?"

I cringed inwardly. The fainting episode was probably

due to the fact that *both* of her parents weren't around. Stress can do weird things.

Chelsea looked at me with pleading eyes. I shook my head to let her know I wouldn't break my promise. The nurse didn't need to know that her mom was missing. Not now. Maybe not ever.

Chelsea opted to stay at school. At lunchtime, I encouraged her to eat even though she said she wasn't hungry. "You don't wanna go falling off any more chairs, do you?"

"I know, I know," she said as we found a table in the cafeteria.

Ashley and Lissa came over and joined us. "How are you feeling?" Ashley inquired. "Did you hit your head?"

"I don't think so." Chelsea felt the back of her head. "Guess I was just so relaxed, I slithered to the floor like a rag doll."

Lissa nodded. "You sure looked like one. I felt so sorry for you. Are you sure you're okay?"

Chelsea muttered something about still not feeling well.

"You look awfully white," Ashley pointed out.

I spoke up, eager to put an end to this worrisome talk. "After a person faints, it takes a while to recuperate." I asked for the ketchup. But Ashley and Lissa kept fussing over Chelsea. Finally, I blurted out, "Does anyone know who Randall Eastman is?"

"Who?" Lissa said.

"Randall Eastman," I repeated. "I heard he's the principal's grandnephew—the student who won first place in the photography contest last year."

Ashley sat up a bit straighter. "*I'd* be interested in meeting him, too. In fact, I'd like to see his award-winning photograph. Do you think maybe we could?"

We?

I sputtered. "Well . . . I don't know. I guess one of us has to track him down first." I felt foolish in spite of the obvious competitive undertow. "Mrs. Fields says he's a junior this year. Anyone know any upperclassmen?"

"Not really," Lissa said. "Maybe some of the guys in the youth group might."

Ashley's eyes lit up. "Oh, what a wonderful idea! That's easy enough. We can ask around on Sunday."

"What about asking Jonathan Klein or his older sister?" Chelsea suggested. "Nikki's a junior this year, I think."

"Hey, your brother oughta know," Lissa said. "Skip took Nikki out several times last school year."

I sighed. "Skip's coming home for the weekend. Maybe I'll ask *him* about Randall Eastman." I turned to look at Chelsea. The color was returning to her cheeks. "Hey, you're starting to look—and sound—more like yourself."

She didn't exactly smile at my observation, but tilted her head modestly my way. "After school I think I'm going to go home and take a long nap."

I wondered about that. "Do you still want me to come over?"

"Sure, why not?"

I couldn't discuss or rehash our sleuthing plans in front of Ashley and Lissa. Still, I wondered if Chelsea was backing out, maybe getting cold feet about gathering clues to find her mom.

Fortunately, I didn't have to wonder long. When Ashley and Lissa finished eating, they excused themselves. At last, Chelsea and I were alone.

"Is it safe to talk now?" I glanced around.

She leaned close, whispering, "I found something in my parents' bedroom this morning."

I was all ears. "Something important?"

"My mom's diary," she said. "I'll show you when you come over."

"That's terrific! Any leads?"

She kept her voice low. "It's hard to say. There's so much repetitious writing in it."

"What do you mean?"

She explained. "The same sentences are written over and over."

"Like what?"

"Things like, *I will turn off my mind and let things float.*"

"Uh-oh." My heart sank.

"What?" Chelsea frowned. "What do you think it means?"

"We really can't be sure, but it sounds almost hypnotic."

"Really?" Chelsea was wide-eyed. "Why would my mom want to hypnotize herself? That's stupid."

"How many times did she write it?"

"Over a hundred, I think."

I shook my head. This was truly frightening. "What about your dad? Does he know what you found?"

"Dad had to leave early this morning to get to the

bank. He's frantic about the missing money. I hated to ask him anything about that strange couple that kept inviting Mom to go places."

"I understand." I sighed as helpless feelings swept over me. "So you must've been snooping around this morning?"

Chelsea nodded. "*That's* why I didn't have time to eat breakfast. I was upstairs in my parents' bedroom, turning the place upside down. I found the diary between the mattresses on Mom's side of the bed." Her eyes glistened. "None of this makes any sense. I'm scared to death."

I wished I could tell her I was trusting God for her, that I was praying, but "Everything's going to be all right" was the only thing I managed to say.

She pushed her long, thick locks off her shoulder. "I sure hope you're right."

I gathered up my trash and stuffed it into my empty cup. "We can't give up. We're just getting started, you know."

She slid her chair back and stood up with her tray. "I know, Mer. Thanks for being there for me."

"Any time."

Together we headed for the kitchen and deposited our trays. Even though Chelsea appeared to be feeling better physically, I knew deep inside she was carrying a sorrowful burden.

I sighed, praying and hoping and counting on God to take away her burden—and to bring Chelsea's mom back home. The sooner, the better!

SEVEN

After school, the long yellow bus automatically stopped near the willow grove on SummerHill Lane.

I called to Mr. Tom, the driver, that I wasn't getting off. "I'm going over to Chelsea's today."

He waved his hand. "No problem!"

When we arrived at the Davises, I spotted a car in the driveway. "Hey, look! Someone's home."

Chelsea groaned. "It's my dad's car. This can't be good news—he's home way too early."

We made our way down the narrow aisle toward the front. The bus door screeched opened and we got off.

"Why do you think your dad's home so early?" I asked as we moved toward the bricked walkway.

Chelsea didn't speak. Her eyes scanned the front of the house.

"I hope it's not about . . ." I didn't finish. No need to heap worry on top of whatever else was flitting through her mind.

"C'mon, Mer." She pulled me around to the side of the house where a massive white ash tree stood sentinel. "We're not going inside just yet. I have an idea."

For a second, I grinned. Chelsea was starting to sound like me. "What's up?" I asked.

She pointed to a slight clearing in the woods behind their house. "Remember the old hut back there? The one that nearly scared us silly when we were kids?"

I strained to see past the thick underbrush, but I knew very well what she was talking about. My childhood memories of the ancient place were clear enough. "What about it?" I said, trying to hide my apprehension.

"Something in Mom's diary makes me think that maybe, just maybe, we might find something important back there in the woods."

"Something important? Like what?" A creepy shiver crept down my spine.

Chelsea turned, heading toward the arbor gate. "Are you coming or not?" Her eyes dared me.

"Look, if we're gonna do some real sleuthing, I oughta have my camera, don't you think?" The thought had literally popped into my head—a clever way to postpone the inevitable moment, perhaps. I kept talking. "That way if we *do* discover something, we'll have proof to show the police or a private investigator."

Chelsea stared at me like I was wacko. "Who said anything about cops? And a private eye—hey, they cost big bucks. Right now, according to my dad, we're broke."

I refused to back down. I wanted my camera—now. "Still, I think it would be smart to take pictures."

We stood under the giant ash, its purple leaves covering us, having our first major standoff. After a few more desperate pleas, Chelsea came to her senses. Maybe she realized I wasn't going to budge. Best of all, she hadn't sensed my uneasiness.

"Why don't you ride my bike down to your house?" she offered, going around to the overhang under the back porch. Her bike was in perfect shape, as though she never, ever rode it.

"You sure?" I asked, noting the fancy leather seat and other expensive touches.

"Go ahead." She parked her books on the patio table nearby, then helped secure my schoolbag on the bike.

"Thanks. I'll be back in a jiffy," I called to her as I pushed off and headed for the driveway.

The distance to my house was all downhill. Coming back, I'd have to pedal hard to make it.

❧   ❧

Mom was cooking something wonderful when I dashed into the house and through the kitchen. "Mm-m, smells great!" I said. "Special dinner for Skip?"

"He should be home soon," she called up the back steps. "What's your hurry?"

"I came home to get my camera," I said, making the conversation up as I went. "Never know when I'll stumble onto a glorious shot."

Mom didn't respond. Either she hadn't heard, or she was already lost in her culinary dreams and schemes. Skip was her one and only son. Naturally, she'd want to knock herself out to make his first homecoming extra-special.

Upstairs, I deposited my schoolbag on the bed, then filled my camera pouch with several new rolls of film. I wanted to be fully prepared. No stones left unturned and all that detective-sounding stuff.

Mom's eyebrows arched when I rushed through the kitchen again, telling her I'd see her later. "Chelsea's expecting me back at her house. We're doing some investigating, I guess you could say."

"Nothing too serious, I hope."

She had me. "Well, maybe. But I won't be long. 'Bye!"

Mom called after me, "Be careful."

"I will," I shouted back. "I promise."

"And be back in time for supper!"

"Okay, Mom."

I made a run for it on the steep hill, but eventually slowed to a turtle trot. My latest mystery—*our* latest mystery—could possibly be wrapped up and solved in one afternoon. That is if Chelsea and I were brave enough to go where the solid leads might be lurking.

I should've been jumping for joy about the prospect of finding Chelsea's mom, but something about the mission made my mouth go dry. It was the old shack. The eerie place out there on the edge of the dark forest.

I licked my lips as I pumped my legs, pedaling for all I was worth. If only we didn't have to deal with the mysterious woods and that hut.

The feverish dryness in my mouth persisted even after I arrived back at Chelsea's house and gulped down a full glass of water in her kitchen.

I gazed through the window at the timberland beyond the rickety arbor gate. In the foreground, tall and wooden, the arbor was cloaked in rambling grapevines now brittle and brown.

The gateway beckoned.

EIGHT

Goose prickles popped out on the back of my neck. I poured more water and drank. The cool water helped—but only for a moment.

Looking out through the kitchen window, I surveyed the fairy-tale entrance to the dark, foreboding forest. The arbor gate seemed to summon me. White stepping-stones, bordered on both sides by a stone foundation wall, scattered away from the arbor, creating a mysterious pathway.

I shivered, thankful for daylight.

Chelsea noticed. "Are you afraid?"

In all the years Chelsea and I had known each other, neither of us had ever stepped foot in the vine-covered shack. The first time I'd ever gotten close enough to investigate, I'd promptly decided it was too far back in the woods for a kids' hideaway. Too far from the safety of the house.

Chelsea, being a timid sort of kid back then, had wholeheartedly agreed.

Better to use it for storing tools and the lawn mower, I'd thought then. But the place hadn't been used that way.

As far as I knew, the vine-tangled shanty had stood empty all these years.

"So . . . are you afraid?" Chelsea repeated, eyeing my camera.

I stood tall, ignoring the question. "Ready?"

"I've got the diary." She held it against her chest. "Now, if I can just find the right page." She glanced toward the living room. "Dad's in there making phone calls, so we'll have to keep our voices down."

"Does he know I'm here?" I leaned around the fridge to peek at him.

"Not really. But if we're quiet . . ." Her voice trailed off, and I struggled to push away creepy thoughts.

Chelsea held the diary open. "Right here." She pointed to a four-line passage that looked like poetry. "I'm pretty sure my mom is referring to the hut out back." She pushed the diary into my hands. "Read it for yourself."

Carefully, I studied the cryptic words.

> *Approach a labyrinth of snarls and tendrils,*
> *Follow the white-stone way.*
> *Spirit-dew, rain on they who here reflect.*
> *House of secrets bids you stay.*

"It's a poem—it rhymes." My lips quivered. "When did your mom start writing poetry?"

"Beats me. Mom's never written any before, at least not that I know of."

Her answer concerned me even more. "Chelsea"—I turned to her, pressing the diary pages shut—"what on earth *is* this writing? These words . . . that spooky stuff

. . . it doesn't feel right to me. I think it might be coming from an evil influence."

She pouted. "You're just saying that so we won't have to go out there and look around."

The tension, the urgency of the situation, made me forget about her dad. "No!" I shouted. "No, that's not it."

"Sh-h! Merry!"

Suddenly, I heard footsteps. "What's all the noise?" Mr. Davis came through the doorway to the kitchen. "Hey, you two having a party without me?" He smiled casually.

"Oh, sorry, Daddy," Chelsea said.

I kept the diary hidden behind my back. "Hello, Mr. Davis. I didn't mean to be so loud."

He ran a hand through his thick graying hair, grunted something, and left the kitchen.

Chelsea motioned me outside on the back porch. "Dad'll probably want to eat supper soon, so we'd better get started. That is, if you're ready?"

I nearly choked. Truthfully, I was glad for the momentary encounter with her dad. Anything to take the edge off what I'd been feeling.

The word *occult* drifted through my thoughts, and although I didn't plan on telling Chelsea about it, I knew I'd have to pray extra-hard tonight. If her mother's mind was being controlled by someone else, someone or something outside herself, we were in big trouble—in way over our heads.

Then unexpectedly—like the swift flutter of wings— a Scripture verse I'd learned as a little girl came to me.

For he will command his angels concerning you to guard you in all your ways . . .

Over and over, the verse echoed in my mind.

He will command his angels . . . to guard you. His angels will guard you. . . . Angels . . .

Adjusting my camera case straps, I moved forward. I glanced around me, wondering, *Are they here? Are God's angels with us now?*

Chelsea followed close behind me, clutching her mother's diary. Together we passed beneath the tall, rectangular arbor gate to get to the white stone pathway.

They will lift you up in their hands, so that you will not strike your foot against a stone.

I looked down at the stony passage leading us to the dark woods, then ahead to the deserted shanty. God had promised to send His angels. They were here.

I wish I weren't, I thought.

Closer, closer we came to the edge of the forest. Dense and foreboding, it loomed ahead like a giant monster waiting to devour us. The sinister-looking hovel came into view as we entered the black woodland, leaving the light of day behind us.

Chelsea's face muscles twitched nervously. "Let's stay together, okay?"

"I'm here" was all I could say. My throat was so dry I could hardly swallow.

Suddenly, she stopped. "Listen!" Her hand trembled—the one holding her mom's diary.

"What is it?" I whispered. "What do you hear?"

Chelsea inched forward. "That sound. . . . What's that weird sound?"

I strained to hear, my knees quaking. "I don't hear anything."

Chelsea turned to me. "Didn't you hear that?"

I listened. Then in the distance, I heard the *snap-a-crack* of a dry twig. I wanted to drop to my knees. "I don't know about you, but I'm going to pray."

"Right here?" Her eyes bugged out.

I nodded.

"But—"

"I'm not going to ask if you mind," I interrupted. "You say you don't believe in God, but I know He's here with us. I also know He wants to help your mom."

She didn't argue this time. I bowed my head and folded my hands with Chelsea's hand stuck between mine. "Lord, we don't know what we're going to find inside this spooky place, but you do. Please keep us safe. And thanks for your angels who protect us. Amen."

Chelsea didn't say a word about the prayer—or the angels. In fact, she was trying to act real cool. But I knew the prayer had touched her. Her eyes were brimming with tears.

Quickly, she turned away. "Okay, let's go," she said.

Help us to do the right thing, Lord, I prayed silently as we moved forward, taking one white stepping-stone at a time.

NINE

Hesitantly, I reached through the vines to unlatch the narrow door. Chelsea held back the thick branches, hands trembling.

"Anyone home?" I called.

We listened.

Nothing. Nothing except the whispery sound of wind high in the trees.

"We're coming in!" I shouted, feeling more confident accompanied by the sound of my voice. With a shove, I opened the door.

There, piled up on the wood floor, were candles—some half burned—two black-and-gold incense containers, and several empty wine bottles.

"What on earth?" I muttered.

Chelsea sniffed the air. "Hey! That's my mom's favorite incense." She picked up one of the round incense holders and held it to her nose. "Weird," she whispered, almost to herself. "I wonder if she's been coming here to meditate."

"Your mom meditates?"

Chelsea was quick to set me straight. "It's *not* what you think, Merry," she said. "My mom's been interested in getting in touch with her inner consciousness for a long time. She likes to spend time concentrating and stuff like that, usually in a quiet place."

"We won't know unless we keep searching." I spied a long black box high atop a potting shelf in the corner. "Look up there," I said, pointing. "What's in that box?"

"Let's check it out."

I dragged a chair under the shelf. Reaching up, I encountered a thick spider web. "Yee-ikes! There are cobwebs all over this place."

Chelsea steadied the rickety chair as she stared up at me. I jumped down, holding the black box, then opened the lid. Inside, we discovered a strange array of items. More candles—mostly black ones—and matches, incense, and several large, black square cloths. And a book with a frightening title: *Taking the Oath*.

A sickening wave of terror welled up in me. "Oh, Chelsea, I think your mom's hooked up with something truly dangerous!"

"Why?" She picked up the book and flipped through the pages. "Because of this?"

The hair on the back of my neck prickled, and I wanted to run. Anything to escape the oppressive sensation that seemed to hover around us.

I noticed some strange markings on the inside of the box but said nothing. By the looks of things, Chelsea's mom had been using the abandoned shack as a hideaway—a place to practice her occult exercises in privacy.

Quickly, I replaced the lid on the box and returned it to its original place, deliberately avoiding annoying spider webs.

Leaping down off the chair, I glanced around at the inside of the hut—about the size of a large bedroom. Fighting off nightmarish feelings, I aimed my camera, taking several shots of the bizarre surroundings before closing the door and latching it.

"Is this building on your property?" I asked as we hurried away.

"It's been here as long as we have," Chelsea replied. "So it must be."

"You're sure it's not on your neighbor's property line?"

"Positive."

I wanted to make sure we weren't trespassing. There was a strong possibility I'd want to return.

"Let me see that poem your mom wrote again," I said.

Chelsea handed the diary to me, and I thumbed through the pages till I found the peculiar poem.

> *Approach a labyrinth of snarls and tendrils,*
> *Follow the white-stone way.*
> *Spirit-dew, rain on they who here reflect.*
> *House of secrets bids you stay.*

I stared at the diary entry. "That's it! The hut has to be the house of secrets," I blurted. "Look, Chels, it's right here." I pointed to the page.

She stopped cold, and I reread the words to her.

"Do you think. . . ? Could it be?" Her voice became hysterical. "Do you think my mom's lost her mind or something?"

"I hope not." What else could I say? The signs pointed to . . . what? I didn't know. But whatever was in that place and in that black box surely wasn't meant for the praise and worship of God.

We quickened our pace, never looking back. I stuffed the diary into my back pocket.

Chelsea's wheezy breathing worried me as our feet flew over the white stones, through the opening in the arbor gate, and back to the safety of her yard.

"Whew, we're back." She collapsed on one of the patio chairs on the back porch. "I can see why we avoided that wretched place as kids." She was totally freaked.

"I'll get you something to drink," I offered, heading for the kitchen door.

Chelsea looked too pale to get up. "I'll be right there."

"Just take it easy," I called over my shoulder.

Inside, I let the water run so it would be cool without ice. Sometimes Chelsea had asthma flare-ups, and I knew better than to give her ice water. I wandered over to the cupboard, searching for a clean glass, when I heard startling words coming from the living room.

"What do you mean, you're not coming home?" Mr. Davis was saying.

I held my breath, listening as I hugged the door frame.

"Where are you now? Where is our money?"

A long pause.

"But that money belonged to me, too," he insisted. "We had plans for that account, you and I—we . . ."

My heart ached for Chelsea's dad. Evidently, Mrs. Davis was on the line. Would she tell him where she was? Why she'd left?

"Please come home, Berta Jean. This is craziness, every last bit of it. Those people, they're nuts and you know it. Why, those crazy mixed-up notions about making the world a better place—and that hocus-pocus non-sense, c'mon!"

Silence again.

Then—"But how can you up and leave Chelsea and me for a bunch of crackpots?" Mr. Davis was weeping now.

Another long pause.

His voice came softly now. "I love you, Berta, don't you see? I want you here, to live with our daughter and me. . . ."

I backed into the kitchen, hurrying to turn off the water. Once again, I felt helpless and frightened for my friend and her father. The pleading continued, but I stood in the kitchen wrapping my arms around myself—trying desperately to block out the frantic words.

"What's that?" Mr. Davis howled. "Me, come and join that weird bunch? Why, Berta Jean, that's ridiculous. I wouldn't think of leaving my life behind for that oath-taking baloney. How can *you*?"

I fought back tears and hurried outdoors with the glass of water. By the time Chelsea was ready to come indoors, the phone conversation had come to an abrupt end. It wasn't my place to fill her in. I shouldn't have heard any of it in the first place.

"You okay?" I asked, watching my friend closely.

She steadied herself against the kitchen counter. "I'm so mad I can hardly stand up," she admitted. "All the weird stuff. Mom's totally flipped—hiding out in that shed and so close to our house."

"It's not *that* close." I glanced out the window. "You can hardly see it from here."

She came over and stood beside me, still wheezing

slightly. "I guess you're right but . . ." She stared out the window, wearing a troubled look. "You don't think . . . my mom's not living out there, is she?"

"There's no evidence of a bed or anything." I thought about the candles and the incense. But it was the book with the frightening title that concerned me most. "No, Chelsea, I don't think your mom's staying there."

"I sure hope not," she whispered, forcing her gaze away from the window.

I gave her a quick hug good-bye. "I think it's time you talked to your dad, though. Just the two of you."

Her father came into the kitchen looking dejected. Chelsea looked at him, then rushed over to him, crying. They scarcely noticed as I slipped out the back door.

The sun was slipping fast over the horizon as I ran down the dirt lane. I held on to my camera case, keeping it from flopping.

Lights twinkled in the downstairs windows of my house just ahead. How I welcomed their golden glow!

At the intersection of Strawberry Lane and SummerHill, I ran across the street, then darted up the long, sloping side lawn, past the grand white gazebo centered in our backyard, and onto the back steps.

It wasn't until I was washing my hands for supper that I realized I hadn't returned the diary. The hard, fat lump protruded out of my back pocket.

Chelsea's mom had been writing bizarre things in her daily entries, that was true. I could only hope that by snooping just a little, perhaps I'd find additional clues.

Where *was* Chelsea's mom?

TEN

Supper by candlelight meant one of two things at our house: Either we were entertaining company, or it was a holiday.

Mom had a funny way of connecting with holidays—even the insignificant ones. They were her excuse to show off culinary skills, not to mention her fine hostess abilities.

But a linen-and-lace tablecloth and napkins on the first Friday in October by no means represented a holiday, significant or otherwise. It wasn't even a full moon.

But it *was* a special event—Skip's first weekend home since we'd bid him farewell on that hot, sweltering day in August.

"How's college treating you?" Dad asked, slapping Skip's shoulder playfully as the two of them wandered into the dining room.

"I like it just fine," Skip said, his face shiny and hair still damp from his shower. Mom always liked it when we freshened up before mealtime. Besides, Skip probably needed freshening up—he'd driven many miles in order to put his feet under her table.

We sat opposite each other, Skip and I. Dad's easy-going grin stretched from ear to ear as he settled into his usual spot at the head of the table. Mom sat at the far end across from Dad, nearest the kitchen. Dad prayed, thanking the Lord for Skip's safe return, then the food was passed. Prime rib, mashed potatoes and gravy, dried-corn casserole, sweet baby peas, homemade biscuits and butter—the works. Once again, Mom had knocked herself out for us. For Skip, really.

Halfway through supper, I asked Skip if he knew who Randall Eastman was. "Supposedly he won first place in the photography contest last year."

Skip glanced at the ceiling, thinking. "Oh yeah, I remember hearing something about that. Isn't he the principal's nephew or something?"

"Something like that." I couldn't believe he hadn't paid attention to last year's contest. Having a sister who was a camera fanatic ought to have tuned him in at least a little. "So do you know him?" I persisted.

"Barely." He pulled on his open shirt collar. "Seems to me the guy's a loner. A little nerdy, too."

"That figures," I sneered. "Most artists are truly misunderstood."

He shot back, "Well, you oughta know." Skip was taunting me. I wished he'd stayed at college.

Mom leaned forward, reaching for my hand. "Oh, honey, that's not how we think of *you*." She'd always been quick to qualify off-the-wall statements by her firstborn. Especially those directed at me. Or Faithie. Except that my twin sister hadn't lived long enough to experience the enduring quality of our big brother's flapping tongue. I was almost positive if Faithie were alive today, she would be even less tolerant of Skip's constant condemnation.

"You just have to have someone to pick on," I muttered.

Mom eyeballed me. "Your brother's been home less than an hour, and here you are—"

"Hon," Dad intervened as usual. "It's okay. We're all just a little tense from the long week. The kids, too."

"Yeah," Skip said, hopping on Dad's bandwagon. "Let's cool it, okay?"

I wanted to bop him good. How was it that he could get by with derogatory comments? This was firstborn ballyhoo at its best!

Mom and I cleared the table, letting the men in the family sit around and twiddle their thumbs. The way I saw it, if Dad had truly had a say in serious table etiquette, he would've been up helping us by now. He didn't strike me as the kind of guy who insisted on being served by females. Never had.

But Skip? My brother simply adored being waited on. Hand, foot, *and* mouth. I, despising the submissive younger-sister role, had made a point of sidestepping the issue as much as possible. With him at least.

The festive dinner tapers had burned down about an inch when Mom and I brought in her cream cake. Made with sweet milk from the Zooks' dairy, the dessert was unbelievably rich. The cream filling alone was outrageous. Dad's cousin Hazel had once called the sumptuous dessert sinful due to its extravagant fattening ingredients.

"Well," Dad said, eyes shining in anticipation, "shall

we ask the blessing once again?"

Mom giggled like a schoolgirl. "You may, if you like."

"Oh, Dad, please," I groaned.

Skip joined Dad in rubbing his stomach and, in general, hammed it up.

Dad was on his second cup of coffee when Skip started telling about some of the extracurricular activities on campus. "You name it, we've got it," he said with pride. "Several Bible study groups meet after hours. One in particular is kinda cool."

Dad's cup clinked as he placed it back on the saucer. "Let's hear about it, son."

I knew I'd be required to stay put and listen, even though Skip's idea of captivating conversation was about as interesting as a car mechanics manual.

After another ten minutes of college talk, I excused myself. "I'll start loading the dishwasher."

Mom nodded silently.

Unfortunately, I could still hear Skip's voice even as I made the usual kitchen clean-up noises. I drew the hot water for the silverware. Never in a million years would Mom allow the dishwasher to clean her good stuff. So I washed the flatware by hand, beginning with the spoons.

Dad's comments floated into the kitchen. "Sounds like a simple case of first-semester blues," he was telling Skip. "You'll survive it, son. Give it a few more months."

Without help from Mom, I finished off the work in the kitchen, even the pots and pans. I was on my way upstairs, heading to my room to tackle homework, when I thought of Chelsea. I said a prayer for her and her family, then worked on history questions until I got stuck.

Quickly, I went back downstairs to ask Dad about it.

In fifteen minutes, I had my answer and was scurrying to my room when I nearly collided with my brother. He was coming down the hall, waving his portable phone. "Was my little Merry hiding the phone?" he taunted.

I lunged at him. "Were you in my room? You know better! And don't call me your little Merry!"

Playfully, he pushed me away. "Hey, relax, cat breath." He shoved the phone into his back pocket. "Don't freak out."

"Stay out of my room, you hear?" I shouted, turning on my heel and slamming my bedroom door.

Mom came up in a few minutes, inquiring about the racket. "I want the two of you to stay away from each other," she said as we stood in the hallway.

I glanced at Skip. "For the whole weekend?" I hoped she meant it.

"We'll have to wait and see." Before she said more, Skip, sporting a smirk, disappeared into his room. "Now, Merry," Mom continued, "your brother's home for a reason. He's tired and was severely homesick, so I want you to ease up on him. Please?"

"Tell *him* that!"

"Merry? What's bothering you?" She forced a smile, looking concerned.

I fought my anger over Skip coming home and barging back into my life. I struggled with feelings of helplessness over Chelsea's mother. Where was she? How could she leave her family? I hated the lump in my throat.

Then I did an impulsive thing. I threw myself into Mom's arms.

"Merry, honey, what's wrong?" She held me close.

I cried as though my heart would break. Actually, it *was* breaking. Breaking for my friend Chelsea and the horrible thing she was going through.

Before too many more seconds passed, I broke free of Mom's embrace (without telling her a thing) and made a beeline to my room. There, I cried my eyes out in private.

ELEVEN

Thank goodness Mom didn't hound me about being upset. She was smart that way. She'd learned not to push things with me when I was off kilter. And it was a good thing, too, because there was no getting around it—I wouldn't break my promise to Chelsea.

Later, when I settled down a bit and my voice didn't sound all crackly from crying, I called Chelsea. "I've been thinking about you," I said, curled up in Dad's comfortable desk chair downstairs. The study was quiet—no chance of being disturbed here.

"I'm glad you called," she said. "My dad and I talked for a long time after you left. And I told him that you knew everything."

"Even about the missing money?"

"That too."

"Is it a problem . . . my knowing?" I asked hesitantly.

"Not really. Dad's so bummed out he couldn't care less who knows anymore. But I'm not just gonna sit around and wait for him to wake up. I'd like to jolt him good."

"What do you mean?"

She sighed. "Oh, Dad's so into himself these days—won't talk much. Withdrawn, I guess you'd say."

"He's mad, probably." *I would be, too*, I thought.

"I've been thinking, Mer. What if we called the cops and reported a missing person?"

"That's a jolt, all right."

"So . . . what do you suggest? Got a better idea?" I could tell she was desperate.

"There *is* something," I said, thinking about the phone call from Chelsea's mom. "You know about your mom's call to your dad today, right?"

"Uh-huh. Dad told me, and he's mighty sick about her attitude."

"Well, what if there'd been a tap on your line when she called? Then the phone company could've traced the call, and we might know where your mom is hiding out!"

"Hey, a genius idea, Mer! When could we get it done?"

"The sooner the better," I suggested.

"But . . . wait a minute. Don't we need to call the police about something like this?"

I gripped the phone. "I don't know. Probably."

"Okay," she said, trying to sound more confident. "I'll call the police department tomorrow morning."

"What about now?" It was a test. I wanted to see how serious she really was.

"Now?" came the raspy reply.

"Sure. Why not?"

There was an unusually long pause. "Well . . . okay, I guess."

"Call me after you talk to the cops," I said.

"Man, Dad's gonna kill me," she whispered.

"Wait till he goes to bed—then call."

"Good idea." She paused for a second. "Could you put the portable phone under your pillow again tonight?"

"I'll see. I'll have to smuggle it out of Skip's room, you know. He's home now and being a bear about it."

"Try really hard. Please?"

"Okay, I'll give it a shot, but knowing Skip, I can't promise anything." I sighed. "Oh, before I hang up, I'd better tell you that I accidentally brought your mom's diary home with me."

"Just bring it over tomorrow."

"I will . . . and Chelsea?"

"Yeah?"

"I wanna go back to the hut again."

"You do? Why?" There was fear in her voice.

"I wanna have another look around."

"Didn't you get enough pictures?" she asked.

"We'll talk about it tomorrow."

"Okay. Thanks for calling, Merry."

"Take care. 'Bye." I hung up feeling closer to Chelsea than ever. Something was different between us. I couldn't put my finger on it, but I sensed it strongly. I was pretty sure when things had begun to change—after the prayer on the stone walkway today. That was it! Chelsea actually seemed different after my prayer.

❧   ❧

I fooled around, watching TV for a while. Skip kept to himself in his room the rest of the evening. Dad and Mom were kind of out of it, too. I didn't blame them for hanging out upstairs in their master bedroom. They had a sitting area in one corner, and I could imagine Mom curled up with a book in her favorite overstuffed chair. Dad was probably already snoozing. He fit the old adage, "Early to bed, early to rise, makes a man healthy, wealthy, and wise."

Around nine-thirty, I felt restless. Nothing good on TV. Hardly ever was. I retreated to my room, calling for my cats to follow but keeping my voice down. Skip was cat-queasy, and the last thing I wanted to deal with to-night was a tongue-lashing about my precious babies.

Once inside my room, the cat quartet knew where to go. My blue comforter was their favorite indoor place to be.

I undressed for bed, looking forward to sleeping in. No school tomorrow—Saturday. I knew I'd have to get up at a fairly decent hour, though. I wanted to start scout-ing out the possibilities for good photography subjects. The contest deadline was one month away, but the way I liked to work, I needed every bit of that time to choose a subject, take various angles, have the film developed, and then select my best work.

All comfy in my long pajamas, I slipped into bed and pulled up the blanket and comforter. My Bible was within reach on the nightstand, but when I stretched my arm, my fingers touched something else: Mrs. Davis's diary.

I picked it up. *Do I dare read it?* I wondered.

Feeling a twinge of guilt, I opened to the first page. The name *Berta Jean Davis* was scrawled across the top. I looked for a phone number or an address but found nothing.

I studied the writing. Since I had no idea how Chelsea's mother usually signed her name, I had no method of comparison. But looking at it now, her signature seemed hurried, almost frantic.

Mrs. Davis had never impressed me as someone in a hurry. She was the epitome of neatness and order. She was a nurse after all, and must've been a very good one to reach administrative levels.

I was about to close the diary and quit my snooping when a tiny set of symbols caught my eye. It was quite difficult to see them—if a person hadn't been caught up in searching out clues as I was, there'd be no spotting them.

Anyway, there in the lower left-hand corner, I noticed the same mysterious marks as I'd seen on the long black box in the shanty hut. Only these had been written upside down.

I stared at them, fighting the urge to record the strange marks on a piece of paper. Hesitating, I wondered if they might be some sort of curse. I cringed at the thought of having the diary inside my house. At night, no less! I abandoned the idea of copying the marks and placed the diary back on my lamp table.

Stress had always triggered hunger pangs in me, so I got up and went to my walk-in closet. There, in several shoe boxes, I had stashed snack food. My own private food pantry. Although Mom thought it was downright silly, she didn't mind. I found some apple-flavored fruit leather to munch on. After brushing my teeth the second time in less than an hour, I reached for my Bible and devotional book, allowing the Scriptures and thoughts for the day to wash over me.

I kept waiting for Chelsea to call. After all, I'd gone to great lengths to get back the portable phone—waiting until Skip was asleep to make my move. Into his room I'd crept, tiptoeing through enemy territory. Silently, I'd snatched the phone off the dresser and padded down the hallway, quiet as a cloud.

Now, the phone lay innocently under my pillow. But it hadn't rung yet, and I seriously doubted if Chelsea had called the police like she'd said she would.

Sleep played tag with me—I was 'it' and couldn't catch her. I turned on my side, thinking of Chelsea Davis and the eerie feeling I'd had as my friend and I stepped gingerly toward the hut. Worse, I remembered Chelsea's dad's persistent pleadings when his wife had called.

The day's images floated over me. I flipped on my back, staring up at the dark ceiling. "Oh, Lord, please do something," I prayed. "Don't let Mrs. Davis get sucked into this . . . this evil hole."

More images. This time, the memory of Chelsea's eyes darting away from mine, tears glistening after my prayer. I felt dizzy. Lying here in my own bed, I felt faint! Yet the more I pushed the images and words away, the more they persisted. *True light . . . resisting the true light. The woods . . . dark, snarling vines . . . the old hut. Black candles . . . incense . . . wine bottles . . . the satanic book . . .*

I rolled over onto my other side as the sights and the sounds of the day poured over me without stopping. At last, I got up and sat on the edge of my bed longing for peace.

"Dear Jesus, I need your help. I can't sleep because of what's happened," I prayed.

In the darkness, I slipped to my knees. "Please, Lord, take care of the Davis family. I can't help them the way you can."

I stopped pleading long enough to thank my heavenly Father. In turn, I was reminded of Psalm 91—the one about the angels. *He will command his angels concerning you to guard you in all your ways. . . .*

I don't know how or when it happened, but I must've crawled back into bed and fallen asleep. Either that or my guardian angels tucked me in. Anyway, I woke up the next morning in bed, having slept soundly, eager to see Chelsea again.

Maybe *today* we'd find her mother!

TWELVE

During Saturday brunch with my family, a phone call came from Ashley Horton. "Merry, guess what I found out?" she said almost before I could say hi. "The guy who won the photography contest last year—you know, that Randall Eastman? Well, he's in Nikki Klein's home-room."

I was flabbergasted. "You called *her* about this?"

"Last night," she admitted, "after I talked to Jon."

Why'd she have to talk to him? I wondered.

She continued. "But the thing is, this guy Randall, he doesn't go by his real name. He has a nickname, and it's really different. Kind of odd."

I wished she'd get to the point. "Yeah, so what's his nickname?"

"Stiggy. His name's Stiggy. Isn't it corny?"

Nobody says corny anymore, I thought, trying to smother my sarcastic thoughts.

"From what Nikki said, I guess Randall's younger brother couldn't pronounce his name when they were growing up." She laughed. "It doesn't figure—I mean, how do you get Stiggy out of Randall?"

"Maybe Randall was stingy growing up," I offered. "Or stinky."

She actually giggled at my remark. Made me wonder why she was acting like this. So jubilant. Unless . . .

"Oh, so you must've *called* Randall . . . er, Stiggy. Right?"

"How'd you guess?" Ashley asked. "Yes, I talked to him, and he says he'll show me his trophy-winning photo sometime next week." She was going way overboard with her enthusiasm.

"That's nice," I said, remembering that it originally had been my idea to meet him. But, not willing to get into a fuss with our pastor's daughter, I let it drop. Who knows, maybe I'd run into Stiggy in the library on the same day he brought his work. And I would certainly know which day that would be. Ashley wasn't very good at keeping things to herself.

"Well, Merry," she was saying, "have you decided what you're going to do for the contest? Or is it a big secret?"

From you it is, I thought, wishing she'd quit asking.

"I have no idea what I'll be photographing. What about you?" I felt I had to show *some* interest.

"Well, I'm torn between several subjects," she explained.

Torn? When was Ashley ever going to come down to earth?

"You don't have to take this contest so seriously," I advised. "It's only a contest."

"Only?"

"Well, you know." I was antsy to get going. I had a

mystery to solve, a life to save . . . and who knows what else might pop up today.

"Only?" she repeated. "How can you possibly say that?"

"Okay, the contest is a big deal," I said. "It only happens once a year." *Now maybe she'll get off my back.*

Mom motioned for me to return to the table.

"I've gotta go, Ashley," I said politely. "See you tomorrow at church."

"Save me a place in Sunday school," she added before saying good-bye. It wasn't actually a command—still, her request bothered me. Was Ashley taking advantage of our one common interest? Make that *interests*—Jonathan Klein was mighty interesting, too.

I went back to my family, who was enjoying a very late breakfast. Mom liked to refer to a meal this late as brunch. It had nothing to do with whether or not we were eating breakfast and lunch-type food combined, just the lateness of the hour.

"Well, what are your plans today?" Dad asked Skip.

"I think I might ride around and see some of my old high school buddies." He leaned back in his chair.

"While you're at it, don't forget Nikki Klein," I teased.

A smile spread across his face. Evidently, there were still strong emotions connected to Jon Klein's sister.

"It's okay if you ask her out while you're here." I grinned. "I'll let you."

"Thanks for your permission, little girl."

Mom's eyes darted between Skip and me. But I didn't

retaliate and turn our playful banter into something Mom needed to referee.

"What about you, Merry?" Dad asked. "What are you doing today?" He delighted in asking questions like this, especially on weekends. For his kids to have definite plans seemed terribly important to Dad.

"I'm going over to Chelsea's, if that's okay."

"How are the Davises doing these days?" Mom asked, picking up several dishes and carrying them to the sink.

"Oh, busy. You know how it is." Vague words.

I thought of the risky prospect of my family hearing about Mrs. Davis on the news or in the papers—especially if Chelsea really *had* gotten the nerve to call the cops.

Yee-ikes, I thought. *Maybe I should change my tune.*

But the more I contemplated the matter, the more confused I became. I could easily bring up the possibility of Chelsea's mom having been engaged in occult practices—meditating in an old, run-down shed strewn with empty alcohol bottles. But what if Dad kept me from spending time with Chelsea today because of it? What if I didn't get another chance to investigate the hut?

Skip and I cleared the table for Mom, which came as a surprise to both her and me. He seemed more like his old self. Maybe he just needed to come home and get a good night's sleep for a change. Maybe his sickness was cured, and he could go back to college—out of my hair!

❧   ❧

The sun was already high when I parked my bike in Chelsea's front yard. She was coming around the side of the house. "Hi," she said, obviously glad to see me. "Did you remember to bring my mom's diary?"

"It's right here." I pulled it out of my back pants pocket. "Did you call the cops?"

She nodded. "This morning—after Daddy left the house. One of the cops I talked to asked if my mom kept a diary." The dark circles under her eyes suggested that she'd slept fitfully or not at all. "They want to look at it." She took the diary from me, fanning through its pages again.

I followed her around to the back porch. "How can the diary help?"

"The police'll compare some of Mom's repetitious writing with that of other known cult members."

"You must've told them a little about her diary."

"Sure did."

"So . . . they probably think she's involved in a cult, right?"

"Maybe." Chelsea pulled on her long, thick ponytail.

"What about the phone tap?"

"An adult has to request it," she said glumly.

"You mean you didn't tell the police that your mom has already called and that she could very well call back?"

"It's no use. Daddy has to be involved, or the phone company won't do it."

"Definitely a problem," I muttered.

Chelsea squinted toward the woods behind their house. "The cops want to get a statement from my dad about Mom's disappearance, but I doubt he'll even talk to them."

"I hope he will," I replied. "When are they coming?"

"In a couple of hours." She frowned, leaning back in the patio chair. "Daddy's not gonna like it one bit."

I snapped open my camera case. "Well, it's the only thing you could do. I mean, we're only kids—we can't stay on the trail of a missing person forever. We don't even drive a car yet."

Chelsea pushed her bangs off her forehead. "Remember how you wanted to go back and have another look at the hut?" Her eyes widened. "Let's go now."

"Okay!" I was eager for this second chance to snoop.

Chelsea put her mom's diary in the house, then we headed for the arbor gate, down the white stepping-stone path to the mysterious shanty. Cautiously, we approached the old place, surrounded by towering trees.

Chelsea waited behind the trunk of a tree several yards back. Glancing around, she called in a whispery voice, "It's awfully dark in here. Let's hurry!"

I took two steps forward, staring into the darkness around me. Then I stopped, captured by the shanty's haunting image just ahead. I groped for my camera.

"This is genius," I muttered to myself. Instantly, I targeted my subject matter for the photography contest. Now, if I could just get the correct lighting—what there was of it. In the dim and shadowy underbrush, I fussed with my camera, setting the lens and the aperture. "Hold on, Chels." I stepped back, steadying myself with my left foot. "I've found a shot too incredible to pass up."

The hut was covered on one side with a tangled maze of ivy dappled in a single shaft of sunlight. I'd seen paintings similar to this—depicting lavish light and contrasting shadow—but never anything like this in real life!

My heart pounded as I steadied my camera. It was truly marvelous the way the sun cast its brilliant luster over the place. *House of secrets*, Chelsea's mom had called it in her strange poem. The occult-ridden hut, now bathed in light, stood for something else in my mind—something other than witchcraft and hocus-pocus. The white light above the roof of the hut represented overcoming evil with good. I laughed out loud, dispelling my fears.

"I think I've found a winning photograph!" I called to Chelsea, considering various angles. Then, stepping closer, I turned the camera on its side for several vertical shots, taking one picture after another.

She shouted back, "C'mon, Mer. What are you doing?" Her voice sounded frantic.

"I'm finished now. Honest." I slipped my camera back inside its case and turned to see her crouched near the base of the giant tree. "You okay?"

"I hate it here." She gazed nervously into the shadows. "I'm . . . I'm really scared."

"Come with me," I insisted.

"No, you go. I'm staying right here."

"I'll hurry, I promise. You stand guard, okay?" I called over my shoulder. "If you see something . . . or someone, just whistle. I'll come running."

That settled, I moved forward, fighting off yesterday's tormenting visions. As I came within inches of the narrow door, I noticed a frightening thing.

The latch. It was hanging open!

Firmly, I placed my hand flat on the door and pushed. It was hard to see inside. There were no lights, not even a lantern. I groped for my camera, preparing for some super-sleuthing shots.

Within seconds, my eyes began to adjust to the dim surroundings, and the first thing I noticed was the vacant spot where the candles and incense holders had been yesterday. I searched the area around me. My eyes scanned the old potting shelf high on the wall.

Empty.

The black box?

Gone!

My hands turned clammy. "Someone's been here. Someone must've seen us yesterday." I spun around, heart in my throat, leaving the shanty door gaping open. "Chelsea, let's get out of here!" I called. "Hurry!"

We scrambled out of the forest and into the sunlight. My knees shook as we ran toward the safety of Chelsea's house.

THIRTEEN

A few solemn moments passed before either Chelsea or I could speak.

"Oh, Chelsea," I cried as we dashed toward her backyard. "Do you think your mom saw us snooping yesterday? Do you think we scared her away?"

Chelsea's mouth twitched. "I . . . I hope not."

"What can we do now?" I groaned. "We were getting so close, and now this!" I remembered that the police were supposed to be showing up soon. "Do you want me to wait here with you for the cops?"

We collapsed into a matching pair of cedar patio chairs. Chelsea pulled out a tissue from her pants pocket and blew her nose. "Mom might've been nearby. Maybe she even saw us go into the hut. Oh, Merry!" She began to sob.

I got up and went over to her, touching her shoulders. "I'm so sorry. I'm truly sorry."

Suddenly, she looked up through her tears. "You know what I wish? I wish your prayers were actually going somewhere. I guess I . . ." She stopped for a second. "I wish there really was a God."

I studied my friend as I sat on the arm of the other patio chair. The physical similarities were strong between Chelsea and her father. She had his straight nose and rounded chin. Other striking resemblances were evident—the way her left eyebrow arched slightly upward and the rich color of her auburn hair.

"Have you ever heard of people being made in God's image?" I asked.

Her eyebrows arched even more. "Not really. Why?"

"The Bible says we are. I guess if you believe God's written words, it's easier to believe His unwritten ones."

She frowned. "I don't get it."

"Look around you, Chels. See the autumn hues on every tree, the flecks of white in the blue sky, the way those grapevines wrap themselves around that old arbor gate?" I hoped I was making sense. "The way I see it, these are God's unwritten words to us. It's like a photographer with a good camera telling a picture essay. You know the old saying, 'a picture is worth a thousand words'?" I played with the camera strap on my case.

Chelsea leaned forward. "So you're saying that nature points us to something or someone who created all this?"

"I'm *sure* it does. Otherwise, nothing else makes sense. Nothing at all."

She turned to me and smiled thoughtfully. "I don't understand half of what you just said, but it sounds nice. I wish it were true."

I didn't have a chance to respond. A squad car was pulling into the driveway. We could see the front end of the hood.

"Come on," Chelsea said. "We have some fast talking to do."

"Yeah. I just hope the cops help us find your mom."

We hurried around the side of the house just as Lissa Vyner's dad was getting out of the car.

"Officer Vyner!" I called to him. "Boy, are we glad to see you."

Chelsea looked confused but somewhat relieved. "I thought . . . uh, I mean, how'd *you* find out about this?"

Officer Vyner explained. "When I heard about your call and what was going on over here, well, I decided I wanted to be the one to handle this one."

"Thanks," I said softly. "It means a lot."

Chelsea nodded soberly. "Finally, someone who'll listen, who'll take this whole thing seriously." And she began to pour out every last detail.

Soon, it was my turn to talk. I told about what Chelsea and I had seen in the old shack yesterday.

Officer Vyner sat on the back porch step, filling out an official report, writing down exactly what we said. I'd never felt so shook-up in my life, but by the time we finished, I was relieved to have shared the secret burden with someone who could truly help.

"Anything else?" he asked, his pen poised in midair. "Is there anything we've overlooked?"

"Well, there *was* something scratched into the bottom of that black box we found," I said. "I saw the exact same thing on the front page of Mrs. Davis's diary."

"Can you describe the markings for me?" Officer Vyner asked as he prepared to take additional notes.

"Would you like to see the diary?" Chelsea asked, looking a bit hesitant.

I nodded, offering moral support. "Good idea."

She went inside and came out quickly.

When the marks were found and scrutinized, I heard Officer Vyner mention the words: satanic cult. The implications of it made me shiver, and while he continued to talk to Chelsea, I went indoors to call my parents. Dad answered on the first ring.

"Could you please come get me?" I asked, now on the verge of tears. "I'm at Chelsea's, and there's something I should've told you . . . uh, before today."

"Honey, are you all right? You sound—"

"Please, just come," I pleaded.

Again he asked. "Merry, honey, are you all right?"

"I'm fine, but hurry."

He said he'd be on his way, and it was comforting to know that there'd be another adult in the house. And soon.

"Thanks, Dad." I shuddered to think how he would feel when he got here and saw the cop car and heard the horrifying story of Chelsea's missing mother.

Quickly, I hung up the phone.

FOURTEEN

Dad arrived a few minutes later looking relaxed and fit in his black sweats—nothing even remotely close to the way he dressed to work at the hospital. Today was one of the few days he'd had off all month. Being the head of the ER trauma team at Lancaster General and on call most of the time made it difficult for Dad to have leisure time.

"What's going on?" he asked as he came up the front steps. He'd arrived before Chelsea's dad, and it was truly a good thing because it gave me a chance—with some help from Chelsea and Officer Vyner—to fill Dad in on exactly what had been going on.

After Dad heard the story, he offered his medical assistance. "I'd be more than happy to help the department in any way," he said, smiling broadly.

"Well, for starters, we'll have the phone line tapped," Officer Vyner informed us.

Chelsea brightened a bit. "You mean, you can do that without my dad requesting it?"

"I'll be talking with your dad soon enough," he said, sliding the clasp on his pen over his shirt pocket.

We heard the sound of tires on the dirt road out front.

"Daddy's home!" Chelsea shouted and ran out to meet him. I was close on her heels, with Dad trailing a few inches behind.

Mr. Davis was clearly surprised to see Officer Vyner and my dad hanging around his house. He eyed Chelsea nervously. "What's going on here?" he grumbled.

Officer Vyner spoke up. "I understand your wife's missing?"

Mr. Davis ignored him and kept walking toward the house.

"Daddy!" Chelsea called. "Please talk to him."

Her father stood still and erect, not moving for a moment as he faced the screen door, perhaps contemplating a response. Then with a grunt, he opened the door and went inside.

"Now what'll we do?" I said, worried for Chelsea.

She scuffed her foot against the dirt—near one of the many flower beds her mom had tended through the years. "Daddy's been like this ever since . . ." She stopped and pulled out her tissue. "What's *wrong* with him?"

Officer Vyner tried to explain. "Your father's hurting, Chelsea. He may be in denial, but no matter what, you must give him your support . . . your love. He needs you now more than ever."

She dried her tears. "What exactly is the occult?" she asked. "Is it the same thing as a cult group?"

Dad was quick to answer her questions. "The words do sound similar, but the occult is most often linked with astrology, psychic prediction, and sometimes magic or witchcraft. The word *cult*, simply stated, means a group of people whose leader persuades the members to believe that he deserves total, unquestioned loyalty and obedience. Sometimes, a cult group may employ occult practices as well."

Dad's gentle eyes studied Chelsea as she stared down at her mother's flower bed, now hard and dry.

"Thanks for coming, Doctor Hanson," she said, turning to face Dad. "And for explaining things."

"We'll be praying that your mother is found soon," Dad told Chelsea as we headed for the car. "Please keep us informed. I know Merry will be in touch, as well."

"Thanks again," she said. "And don't worry about me, Merry. I'll be fine."

I waved to my friend. "I know you will."

Dad opened the car door for me and hurried to get in on the driver's side. Nothing was said about hanging out with the wrong company—none of that. Dad was sweet. He reached over and squeezed my hand. "I'm glad you're all right, dumpling."

He started the car and drove down SummerHill Lane to our house.

"Do you think they'll find Mrs. Davis?" I asked.

Dad glanced at me. "Chelsea and you did the best thing for Mrs. Davis by getting the authorities involved." He explained that there was a special forces unit at the police department. "They have a number of highly trained dogs who can follow car-exhaust fumes and pick up many other kinds of scents."

"Wow, that's incredible. So you think it's possible that Mrs. Davis might be coming home soon?"

Dad shook his head, wearing a gloomy expression. "I didn't say that. You have to realize that members of cult groups lose their ability to rationalize and reason clearly. Their minds become prisoners, controlled by a leader who is often a power-crazed individual."

"Is that what you call brainwashing?" I asked, remembering the repeated sentences in the diary.

"People adhering to mind-controlling practices and, in this case, possibly mystical formulas, often don't realize what's happening until it's too late. Their minds can be trapped in just a short time frame." He steered the car into our driveway.

"Do you really think Chelsea's mom could fall for something like that?" I asked, afraid to hear his answer.

"Didn't Chelsea say that her mom had always been intrigued by the mystical?"

I grimaced, remembering how Mrs. Davis was obsessed by astrology—especially reading her horoscope and forecasting her future. "I'll pray she comes to her senses." I got out of the car, heading for the kitchen door. I hoped Chelsea's mom would be found soon.

My cats were waiting inside. "Hello, babies," I cooed, scooping up Lily White, then turned to Dad as he came in. "Thanks for helping us—Chelsea and me—today."

He nodded. "I only wish you had told your mother and me right away, when you first heard about Mrs. Davis." He lifted the lid on the strawberry-shaped cookie jar and reached in, pulling out two homemade chocolate chip cookies.

I truly hoped getting Dad and Officer Vyner involved might speed up the process of locating Chelsea's mom. I hoped it with everything in me.

FIFTEEN

"Want some Kitty Kisses?" I asked my feline four-some. Abednego, the self-appointed spokescat for the group, licked his chops.

"Okay, that settles it—liver and tuna crunchies coming up." I pinched my nose shut with one hand and reached into the box with the other. "Chow time!" I divvied up the smelly, heart-shaped cat snacks.

That done, I washed my hands and headed out front to get the mail. There was a fat pile waiting, and without glancing through any of it, I hurried into the house.

"Mail call," I said, putting the stack of letters and bills on the corner table in the wide entryway.

Mom emerged from her sewing room looking dazed. She often appeared rather intense when she was designing a pattern for a new outfit. I told her briefly about Chelsea's nightmare and what had transpired in the last several days.

"Merry, honey," she said, pulling on her hair. "You should've told us. Something like this . . . you shouldn't have carried the burden all alone."

I knew she would say something like that. "It's okay,

I guess. I usually learn the hard way."

She was relieved to know that Dad had been up to see the Davis family. "We certainly must follow up on them. Chelsea and her father will need all the emotional support they can get. Plenty of prayer, too."

We talked for a while longer, then I excused myself to go to my room.

I was approaching the top of the long front staircase when Mom called to me. "Merry! I think you'll be very interested in this." She waved a white envelope.

"Is it from Levi?" I asked.

There was a surprising smile on her face. "Looks as though he wrote a Scripture on the back of the envelope."

I flew back down the steps. "Levi loves studying the Bible. He'll make a great preacher someday." I snatched up the letter and darted up the steps, taking two at a time.

Shadrach and Meshach must've taken my galloping as an invitation to follow. Here they came, tearing up the stairs and down the hallway.

"Hurry up, little boys," I said, waiting for them before closing my door.

Ah, privacy. After the hectic, emotional events of yesterday and today, I was more than happy to pack away my camera and settle down with a long letter from Levi Zook. Four hand-written pages!

My dear Merry,

For such a long time, I have been wanting to write to you. Many wonderful-gut things are happening to me here in Virginia. I am excited to be learning how to write and spell better. My English is improving, too, which I

*am thankful for. Also, the way I am understanding the
Scriptures more and more urges me to get out and preach
the Gospel as soon as possible.*

*How are you doing, Merry? Do you enjoy your new
position this year at your high school?*

I chuckled as I read the last sentence. Levi hadn't remembered to call me a freshman. Amish young people
only attended school through the eighth grade, so they
didn't have to bother with class names like we "English"
did in public school.

I eagerly read on.

*Receiving your letters has been very much enjoyed by
me, and I must say that they have helped me learn about
writing my own thoughts more expressively—(I believe
that is the correct adverb).*

*I miss your laughter, Merry, and your bright eyes. If
it is not too much to ask, would you mind sending me a
photo of you? You see, I do not have one, and now that
I am out of the Amish church, I feel it would do me no
harm to carry your picture in my wallet.*

I reread the last paragraph. He wanted my picture for
his wallet!

Suddenly, an overwhelming sense of loss came over
me. I don't know if the sadness was triggered by a delayed
reaction to the dire situation with Chelsea's mother or
what. But a hard, dry lump sprang up in my throat. My
vision blurred, and I reached for the blue-and-white
striped tissue box on the nightstand.

Why was I crying over Levi's letter? This was the boy
I'd grown up with. His Amish culture was as common to

me as the palm of my hand. When he had struggled with his decision to leave the Amish church, I tried to be patient and listen to his reasons. I worried about the consequences. But Levi wanted God's will above all things, so who was I to regret his leaving SummerHill?

Of course, my loss was nothing compared with that of Levi's parents, Abe and Esther. They'd always had high hopes for their next-to-oldest son. As any faithful Old Order Amish mother and father, they longed to see each of their children follow in their footsteps.

But Levi had been rebellious as a child, pushing the limits. He loved learning and books and constantly asked questions, too. None of that set well with the traditional Amish society. Being obedient and submissive to the rules set down by the *Ordnung*—the Amish blueprint for life—was priority in the plain community.

And here I was, missing Levi Zook. Missing him and wishing he were home. Drying my eyes, I continued to read his letter.

> *I hope you will not be very disappointed to know that I am planning to go overseas to help build a church. Because I have not been assigned to a country yet, I cannot tell you where I will be working. I suppose all those years of raising barns in a single day will help me to assist other Christian carpenters.*

My eyes drifted away from the letter. Building a church overseas? This meant that Levi would not be coming home at the end of the first quarter as planned. I wondered when I'd see him again. Thanksgiving? Christmas, maybe?

I was eager to know.

You must please forgive me, Merry, if this news comes as a surprise. We will have many other happy times together, I trust.

But when? If Levi went overseas and got involved in building projects, maybe he'd *never* want to return home.

I finished reading the letter, hoping against hope that he might explain further his decision not to come home in two weeks. But there was no additional explanation.

Feeling empty and filled with questions, I put the letter in my desk drawer and headed over to the Zooks' dairy farm. Maybe Rachel, Levi's younger sister, could explain things. Besides, a visit to my Amish neighbors was sure to do me good.

SIXTEEN

Through the willow grove and past the white picket fence, I flew. The sun cast angular shadows over the meadows as it played peekaboo through a fleeting cloud.

Rachel was outside beating rugs with her sisters, Nancy and Ella Mae, and they stopped to wave to me. "Hullo," they called in unison as I sprinted across the meadow toward the old white farmhouse.

The girls wore long brown work dresses with buttonless gray aprons over the top, fastened in the back with straight pins. The strings on their white-netting prayer *kapps* flapped in the breeze.

"Looks like someone's having house church tomorrow," I said, running up to the long front porch.

"*Jah*, it's our turn," Rachel said. "Wanna help?"

"Sure." I picked up a multicolored rag rug and beat it against the porch railing. "Have you heard from Levi lately?"

"Only that he's not comin' home fer a bit." They'd heard about the overseas project, all right.

I sighed. "He must like his new college life."

Rachel nodded, careful not to say too much in front

of her younger sisters. "We miss him around here. 'Specially Dat. He's not as young as he used to be, ya know, and farmin's gettin' to be harder for him."

Especially hard—the way they do it, I thought. Mules instead of tractors, and kerosene or gas lamps instead of electricity. The inconveniences and hardships of Old Order Amish life were mind-boggling.

"I'm thinkin' that Levi's gonna get spoiled," Rachel said. "There's no chance he'll ever come back to farmin'."

"You're probably right," I said, helping the girls carry the rugs inside. I stayed around awhile, mostly to visit with Rachel. She and I hadn't seen each other as much as we liked because of my homework load this semester. Rachel, too, seemed busier now that she was at home all day helping her mother instead of attending school. Sometimes Rachel had to help with the more strenuous outdoor chores, filling in for Levi in his absence.

I wanted to ask her about Matthew Yoder, the Amish carpenter's son down the lane, but no opportunity presented itself. There was simply no discussing such things as boys or romance in front of the rest of the family.

"Let's show Merry our puppies," little Susie said, coming into the kitchen. Her eyes sparkled as she pulled on my hand, leading me out the back door and across the wide yard to the barn.

Rachel, Nancy, and Ella Mae followed exuberantly. Inside the hayloft, on a warm bed of hay, Levi's silky gold cocker spaniel lay sleeping next to her pups.

"Oh, they're beautiful." I crouched down for a closer look at the four golden-haired darlings.

"Wanna take one home?" Susie offered. "Pick out the puppy ya want."

I shook my head reluctantly. "Mom would never stand for it," I confessed. "It would be a waste of time to even try to talk her into it."

Rachel leaned down and picked up one with a hint of a wave in his coat. "This one's my favorite," she said, "but Dat says we hafta give them all away."

Susie poked out her bottom lip. "I wish we could start a puppy farm. Levi and I were gonna have us a fine pup ranch. But he went away."

Rachel put her hand on Susie's head. "Don't fuss over what might've been. We'll find good homes for the pups like Dat says. That's all ya need to think about now."

Soon it was time for the afternoon milking. Since I was already here, I decided to don Levi's old work boots and help out. It felt mighty strange clumping around in the mud and manure wearing my former boyfriend's boots. Memories of last summer filled my mind with warm, cheerful thoughts as I washed down the cows' udders in preparation for milking.

Levi and I had pretty much turned things upside down last summer. My own parents had more than raised an eyebrow when I'd consented to spend time with an Amish boy. Mom's concern was that plain folk often marry young. *Next thing, Levi will be looking for a wife,* Mom had said.

Dad, on the other hand, was more nonchalant about Levi's interest in me. *It's not like Merry's going out with some stranger,* he'd said, laughing.

Dad was right. Levi and I were family in a very distant

sort of way. One of my great-great-grandfathers was one of Levi's ancestors, too.

After nearly two hours of rolling the metal milk cans back and forth to the milk house, I was quite exhausted. The Zook kids set high standards for themselves, however, and kept going. They were used to it, though, up at four-thirty each morning milking and hauling the fresh milk out to the end of their lane for the milk truck.

"I'll come see you again soon," I called to Rachel as her father shuffled into the barn. Now was a good time to exit since Abe would help finish up. I removed the familiar work boots and waved good-bye, wondering how long before Levi would miss the old home place. Or if he would at all.

❧   ❧

Right before supper, Chelsea called. I was in no mood for more bad news, so I took the phone somewhat reluctantly. "Hi, Chelsea," I said. "What's up?"

"You'll never believe this," she began. "The police have already found evidence to prove that there are other members of a satanic group in the area. It is a definite cult group—could be the one my mom's hooked up with."

"Wow, fast work. Now, if they can just find your mom and get her out of there."

"I know," she said. "Hey, my dad's coming around—finally! He's been talking to the police. Officer Vyner's been incredible. He told Daddy that they were able to track down several information files in the Lancaster newspapers. The media might be able to help us, too."

Chelsea sounded upbeat and excited. "I guess sometimes bad stuff can turn out to be good—in a way," she added.

"You're right," I replied, hoping this was one of those good times.

"And, Merry, I think you might be the reason for it."

"Me?"

"Your prayer that day, remember?" She said it softly. "You got me thinking about God—angels too—especially being scared spitless out there in the woods."

I hardly knew what to say. Chelsea had never shown any interest in God or His angels.

She changed the subject and chattered about school and boys, and even her algebra homework. Eventually, we said good-bye and hung up.

I pranced back into the kitchen with the phone cord dancing behind me. "Things are looking up for Chelsea and her family," I informed everyone.

"Prayer makes a difference," Dad was quick to say.

"Sure does," Skip said.

My head jerked up as I looked at him across the table. "You're praying, too?" I asked Skip, who'd heard about Chelsea's mom in only the past few hours.

"Mrs. Davis can't begin to know what she's up against with all of us praying," Skip said. It was the one serious comment he'd made all weekend.

Funny thing—my brother didn't pick a single fight at this meal. Not one.

SEVENTEEN

I didn't purposely save a seat for Ashley Horton in Sunday school the next day. At least, I didn't go out of my way to. But there it was, a vacant seat next to me just the same, and she spied it when she arrived.

Ashley made quite a production out of getting from the doorway to her seat. "Oh, Merry, you remembered," she acknowledged, prancing over to me. "Thank you so much." She sat beside me, smoothing out her dress and looking down at her nylons—I don't know why—maybe to make sure there were no runs, heaven forbid.

She certainly accomplished what she'd set out to do. There wasn't a single set of male eyeballs in the classroom who'd missed her entrance. Jon Klein's included.

"I heard about Chelsea's mom on the news last night," she said.

By now, several other kids had come over to discuss the horrendous situation. Lissa too.

"What was all that about Chelsea's mom being involved in a cult?" Lissa asked.

"It's a frightening thing," I said, trying to explain everything quickly before the teacher arrived, "but I believe God will take care of Mrs. Davis."

Jon came over and sat in front of us. Ashley nearly died on the spot. I, however, remained cool and calm. Collected? Not on the inside!

Fortunately, the Alliteration Wizard didn't spring something on me right there in front of everyone. I probably wouldn't have been able to think fast enough. Besides, I loved the fact that he was keeping our word game hush-hush.

After all the talk about Chelsea's mom and her disappearance tapered off, Ashley asked me quietly about the photography contest. Again.

"So . . . have you decided anything yet?" she asked.

Jon had turned around in his seat and was grinning at me. I smiled back. "Oh, that . . . the contest."

"Well," she huffed, "isn't it about time to make some sort of decision?"

"Probably." I was being evasive and she knew it, but I didn't dare share my photography idea with anyone. Especially not with Ashley Horton. Next thing, she'd be out tramping around the woods near Chelsea's house, searching for an old shanty with a beam of light pouring down out of the sky.

Jon turned around, and I opened my Bible, looking for my notes. I'd actually written notes on the lesson for today. Not something I often did, but the trauma of the weekend had served to put my mind on the things of God. Tragedy has a way of doing that. Besides, today's lesson was about angels.

Mr. Burg showed up right on time. His blond hair was accentuated by his gold and blue paisley tie. "Good morning, class." He smiled warmly. "Today we're going to discuss God's unseen protectors."

I opened my Sunday school lesson book so I could follow along. Mr. Burg started the class with prayer and then recited various documented stories about intervention by angels. I was fascinated, remembering how the Lord had dropped the verse from Psalm 91 into my heart last Friday. In that chilling moment, I'd prayed on my knees—in front of Chelsea, the self-declared atheist.

What made me do such a thing? Thinking back, I knew I'd done the wise thing.

Ashley's Sunday school lesson slid off her lap, startling me back to the discussion at hand. The book conveniently landed under Jon's chair. Not surprisingly, he leaned over and reached back to pick it up. Ashley literally gushed her whispered thanks, and I felt embarrassed to be sitting next to her. The girl was overbearing and obviously determined to get Jon's attention. No matter what.

I could only hope he would remember who his equal was in the world of words. Merry, mistress of mirth, made the maddening, maladjusted maiden, Ashley, seem meaningless by a major margin. Or so I hoped.

❧   ❧

Monday morning before school, I dropped off my roll of film at the photo lab. Skip had decided to stay an extra day before heading back to college, and I was shocked when he offered to drive me to school. I must admit, it was nice having him behave so brotherly.

I knew he would be gone by the time I arrived home

that afternoon. "I hope things go okay for you at school," I ventured, tiptoeing around the fact of his former homesickness.

His smile reassured me. "Dad talked to me—said I could come home any old weekend I wanted." He waited for the red light two blocks from Buchanan High, turning in the driver's seat to look at me. "I'll be praying for your girlfriend's mother," he said softly.

"Sounds to me like she needs all the prayers she can get," I replied.

Skip continued. "Well, I'm glad Chelsea has a friend like my little Merry."

He'd called me that ever since I could remember. At least today he'd abandoned "cat breath"—the nerdy nickname he often called me.

Grinning, Skip pulled up to the curb. "Well, here you are."

"Thanks for the ride."

He poked my arm playfully. "See ya at Thanksgiving."

"Yeah, see ya. 'Bye!" I jumped out of the car and watched him drive away. Thank goodness he'd begun to show signs of actual reform. Could it be that my brother and I might someday enjoy a decent sibling relationship?

I hurried up the steps to the school, anxious to turn in my application for the photography contest. Even before stopping at my locker, I dashed down the hall to Mrs. Fields's homeroom. No one was there, but I noticed that someone had already returned an application. I leaned over, studying the paper on the desk. Lissa Vyner's name was at the top. I wondered if Ashley Horton would be turning in her application early, too. Since she was in another homeroom, I had no way of knowing.

Later, right before Mr. Eastman came over the intercom with his usual boring remarks about the day, I passed a note to Lissa.

> *Hey!*
>> *I see you turned in your photo contest stuff early—just like me. Any idea what Ashley's up to?*
>>
>>> *—Mer*

Lissa wrote right back—during the long verses of the national anthem. I remembered what Mom had said about Mr. Eastman, our principal and hers, bellowing out "The Star-Spangled Banner" way back when.

> *Mer,*
>> *You've been snooping on me, huh? Personally, I don't know what's with Ashley these days. I suspect she's planning to get some ideas from that guy, Stiggy Eastman—you know, last year's winner?*
>> *Let's eat lunch with her today and check it out.*
>>
>>> *Later,*
>>> *Lissa*

❧　　❧

It didn't take long to figure out Ashley's next move. She spelled it right out for us over hamburgers.

"Stiggy's been so helpful," she announced to Lissa, Chelsea, and me. "You should hear him talk about things like the composition of the shot, and—oh yes, the most striking element of a scene. I'm really impressed, even though I won't be viewing the winning photograph until Wednesday."

Wednesday!

Even though Ashley didn't bother to invite either Lissa or me to tag along, we weren't going to pass up the chance to have a look. We'd just have to concoct our own plan.

"By the way, have the police followed up any more on your mom and that cult she's in?" Ashley asked Chelsea.

"They're getting close." Chelsea cast an insightful glance my way. "And my mom called late last night."

I gasped. "Did they trace the call?"

"She was calling from a fitness gym somewhere west of town" came the disappointing words. "At least we know she's still in the state."

"Maybe she'll call again," I offered, hoping to comfort my friend.

Ashley's eyes widened. "Well, I certainly hope so. Everyone at church is praying that she'll come home soon."

I wanted to say, *Be careful how much you tell her* but spooned up some applesauce instead. Only God knew whether Mrs. Davis would come home soon or not. And He certainly wasn't to be underestimated. Not in the least!

EIGHTEEN

The next day, Tuesday, Lissa and I sat together in study hall. We ended up passing notes, working out a plan for gracefully bumping into Stiggy Eastman and his wonderful award-winning photography. Tomorrow!

For me, it really didn't matter much, mainly because I was fairly certain my own subject matter was superb. The unusual spiral-shaped beam of light hovering over the old hut quite possibly made my photos superior. I wouldn't know for sure until I picked up my film after school.

Lissa was mighty charged up about seeing the kind of competition we were up against. She whispered to me when the teacher wasn't looking. "If Stiggy's work was really incredible, you know the judges will be looking for more of the same quality this year."

She was right. "Don't worry, just do your best," I advised, deciding to cool it and get to work. The study hall teacher was beginning to scowl; her eyes glared a warning.

I mumbled a barely audible sound, and Lissa knew that, for now, our conversation was history.

The time passed quickly, and soon the dismissal bell rang. I walked with Lissa to her locker in the middle of an ocean of kids.

"Mind if I tag along to the photo lab with you?" she asked, twirling her combination lock.

I smirked. "You're kidding, right?"

"I'm serious. I wanna see my competition."

"It's probably not a good idea," I said, stalling—hoping she'd drop the subject. "You know how I am about this. If I show you, then Chelsea and Ashley . . . *everyone* will want to be in on it."

Lissa's eyelids fluttered upward in disgust. "C'mon, Mer, no one else has to see."

I shook my head. "Can't."

"Why, 'cause you think your pictures are so good?" There was a touch of sarcasm in her voice.

"Actually, you never know," I replied. "My lighting could be all wrong." It was true—the lighting had been tricky that day—the one thing that most concerned me about the shoot.

"Well, have it your way." She reached for her books and slammed her locker.

Chelsea came over with several other girls. "Riding the bus home?" she asked me.

"I plan to if I get back from the photo lab in time."

Chelsea's face lit up. "Oh yeah, I wanna see your pictures."

I was afraid of this. Chelsea was the only person who knew about my subject matter for the contest—that is, *if* she'd paid attention that day in the forest. I couldn't be totally certain, though. Chelsea had been literally freak-ing out behind the tree trunk.

Lissa leaned against her locker, her arms crossed, waiting for my reply. She would be hurt if I gave in to Chelsea's request, ignoring hers.

"Tell you what," I said. "I'd better pick up my film all by my lonesome. That way no one'll feel left out." I shot a sympathetic smile at Lissa, who pinched up her face in response.

"Aw, Mer!" Chelsea wailed.

Lissa leaned forward. "It's okay—we'll get to see Merry's incredible work soon enough."

Lissa and Chelsea were still yakking when I excused myself and slipped away to the photo lab down the street.

№   №

The white-haired man behind the counter seemed a bit confused. "How many rolls of film did you say?"

"Only one—twenty-four exposures."

He searched through the alphabetized packages for the second time, humming off-key as he did. I could see that he was coming to the end of the stack, and my throat felt tight.

"Excuse me," I ventured. "Is the lady here, the one who took my film yesterday?"

The old gentleman shook his head. "I'm sorry, young lady, but that was the manager's wife, and she and her hubby are off to New York City on a business trip."

"I see."

What experience does he have running the place? I wondered.

"But not to worry," he added. "I'm fairly certain your pictures will turn up."

Fairly certain? Yee-ikes!

He opened a drawer and pulled out a pad and pencil. "Let's have your address and phone number."

"Uh . . . sir, you don't understand," I said, willing the panic out of my throat. "I *have* to get those pictures back. It's important . . . for a school photography contest."

His watery blue eyes seemed to register my concern. "I'll call you the minute I locate them."

"Where else might they be?" I persisted, trying to sound mature about this despite the knot in my stomach.

"Wait right here." He turned and shuffled off toward the back room.

Peering over the counter, I read the upside-down names on the packages. I was clear up to the *d*'s when he returned. Stepping away from the counter, I noticed his hands were empty.

"No such luck." He tilted his head to the side, and his hands flew up in front of his face. "I did all I know to do, but"—and here he sighed—"I'll keep tracking them for you."

"Please, will you call me the minute you know something?" I pleaded, then turned to leave.

"I certainly will."

He waved. I didn't.

The sun cast intermittent splotches of light along the sidewalk as I hurried back to the school. "I can't believe this," I muttered as the frustration mounted inside me. I took the steps to the high school two at a time.

Chelsea was coming out one of the front doors as I

pushed on the metal bar opposite her. "Oh, Mer, there you are," she greeted me, eyes searching. "How'd your pictures turn out?"

"Don't ask." I shrugged. "They're lost."

"They're *what*?" She started to follow me inside.

I put up a hand. "Hold the bus for me. I just have to pick up my English notebook and some other stuff."

"You got it." She turned and headed back outside.

The semi-empty building seemed almost hollow, reminding me of the afternoon Chelsea had first told me the startling news about her mom.

Dashing through the hallways toward my locker, I took note of the muted sounds my tennies made in the hushed corridor. Quickly, I passed the many narrow rows where the upperclassmen had been assigned lockers earlier in the year.

Someone was whispering down the hall. "Oh, Jonathan, how funny!" A tight little laugh followed.

I rotated my combination lock. *Click.* Then cautiously, I glanced over my shoulder and pulled down on the lock at the same time.

Two people, way at the end of the hall, were talking. One was laughing. I heard Jon's name again, and then Jon himself said something. The echo distorted the sound of his voice, so I couldn't make out what the Alliteration Wizard was saying. Not exactly. But there were a few words I did catch—something about helping to set up a photo shoot Friday after school.

I slammed my locker door, the sound reverberating through the vacant hallway. As fast as I could, I ran for the front doors and down the steps.

Chelsea leaned out one of the bus windows, calling to me. "Hurry, Merry!"

Rushing into the bus and up the steps, I stopped to thank the driver before sliding in next to Chelsea.

"Never a problem," Mr. Tom said, reaching for the lever to pull the bus doors closed.

When I looked out the window on Chelsea's right, I noticed Jon Klein strolling out of the building. His eyes spotted the bus, but he turned to speak to a girl—probably the same one who'd been laughing and whispering his name in the deserted hallway.

Fuming, I called to the driver. "Better wait. Here come two more stragglers."

Mr. Tom reached for the lever, and the doors screeched open wide. I fumbled for my English notebook, pretending to read as Jon hopped on the bus, followed by none other than Miss Ashley Horton.

NINETEEN

"What happened to your pictures?" Chelsea asked.

I stared down at my English notebook, trying to block out the vision of Jon and Ashley having just boarded the bus. For all I knew, they were sitting together!

"The pictures," Chelsea repeated. "Where are they?"

"No one seems to know," I muttered, not looking up.

"But how could this happen?"

My eyes bored a hole in my notebook.

Chelsea nudged me. "Mer?"

"Never mind," I said through clenched teeth. "And don't turn around if you know what's good for you."

She controlled herself—didn't careen her neck like a giraffe and scope out the situation the way I thought she would. "What's going on?" she whispered.

"Tell you later. Get off with me at my house, okay?" I sounded mechanical through stationary lips.

"Deal," she replied, lips clamped.

We burst out laughing at our robotic antics. I did my best to keep my eyes forward.

Next thing I knew, Lissa showed up and scrunched her thin body in next to mine.

"Hey, *three* don't exactly fit here," I said, squirming.

"Listen, I've got some really good stuff." Lissa bent low, and Chelsea and I matched our heads to hers. "Ashley meets Stiggy Eastman at the sandwich shop tomorrow. Twelve sharp. Be there!" Almost as quickly as she came, she disappeared.

"Oh-ho," I shouted. "I love you, Lissa!"

Chelsea grinned. "What do you care about Stiggy and his work? That's last year's stuff. You've got a fantastic setup for *this* year," she encouraged me.

"Yeah, if the photo lab ever finds it."

"Maybe you should call them again when we get to your house."

I nodded. "Genius."

That's what we did. The minute Chelsea and I walked in the back door, we slipped past the expectant faces of four felines and headed for Dad's study.

After finding the number in the phone book, I dialed the lab. The old guy answered. "Photo lab, may I help you?"

"I hope you can. This is Merry Hanson calling. I wonder if you've been able to find my single roll of developed film."

"*Who* did you say?"

I went through the whole rigmarole again, reminding him who I was, what I wanted, and why I was concerned.

Finally, he said, "Ah yes. I've been trying to phone you, but there's been no answer."

"Well, I just got home," I explained. "So . . . you must've found my pictures." I tingled with excitement.

"Yes, yes, they're here."

"Oh, thank you, sir. I'll pick them up first thing to-morrow." I paused, grinning at Chelsea. Then, turning my attention to the voice on the phone, I said, "You'll hang on to them for me, won't you?"

"I certainly will, young lady. Glad to be of service."

❧   ❧

Actually, when it came right down to it, I couldn't wait to see the photos. The minute Mom arrived, I pleaded with her to drive me down to the photo lab. She had other things on her mind.

"Evidently, you girls haven't heard the latest," Mom was saying.

"About what?" I asked, peering wide-eyed at Chelsea.

"It seems that someone has discovered a page of rep-etitious writing—something similar to your mother's di-ary, Chelsea." Mom looked at her, then me.

"Where?" Chelsea asked.

Mom's eyes shone. "In a gas station somewhere in the area of Mt. Pisgah."

"Really?" I couldn't believe it.

Mom said, "The news report I just heard seems to indicate that a cult group has been located and certain members identified."

"This is so-o incredible!" Chelsea exclaimed.

I gave her a squeeze. "Your dad's probably beside himself, don't you think?"

Chelsea nodded. "I'd really like to go home. Do you mind, Mer?"

"Of course not—you're outta here!" I was delighted.

❧   ❧

Mom drove the short distance up the steep grade and dropped Chelsea off at her house, then headed toward town.

"Do you think this could be the end of the ordeal?" I asked Mom.

Her eyes were thoughtful. "Keep praying. These situations are never open-and-shut cases, as you might think. Chelsea's mother won't come home unless *she* chooses to do so, which is highly unlikely. And that probably won't happen for a long, long time."

I thought about that for a moment. "Wouldn't Mrs. Davis have to be totally brainwashed if she doesn't want to come home? I can't understand it!"

"People—normal, intelligent people—fall prey to cult recruiting every day, Merry." She reached over, resting her hand on my shoulder.

"I just hope someone can help Mrs. Davis." I struggled with desperate feelings.

Mom bit her lower lip. "Your father doesn't offer much hope for her return, at least not of her own free will."

"What are you saying?" My throat felt lumpy again.

"This is absolutely *not* to get out." Mom glanced at me with serious eyes. "You must not breathe a word to Chelsea or to anyone else. Do you understand?"

I nodded, wondering what she would say.

She sighed audibly. "Mr. Davis has been talking with Dad about the possibility of kidnapping his wife and having her deprogrammed and eventually rehabilitated."

I gasped. "Chelsea's dad would kidnap his own wife to get her back?"

"Desperate family members do it all the time."

This was unbelievable. "When will it happen?" I asked.

"I don't know for sure, but I think it will be soon. The longer he waits, the longer her rehabilitation could be."

"But it's only been five days since she left," I said.

"Five days of living with a power-crazed leader who orders everything his followers do and sometimes say—from their bedtimes to the amount of hours they're permitted to sleep, to the way they interact with each other, to what they eat. . . ."

I got the picture. Besides that, I remembered Chelsea hinting that the mind-controlling techniques had probably started weeks before her mom ever left. And there was Mrs. Davis's long-standing fascination with the occult.

The photo lab was within view now. I thought about the things Mom had told me as she pulled up to the curb and parked. "I'll wait for you here," she said.

I hopped out, feeling a bit numb. Yet I was eager to lay eyes on my options for the photo contest. Quickly, I closed the car door and headed toward the shop.

Inside, no one was tending the register. I waited impatiently for several minutes before I rang the bell on the counter.

The old man peeked around the corner, smiled a grin of recognition, and lumbered across the room. "Yes, yes," he said. "You're the young lady who called."

I nodded, dying to get my hands on the photos.

He thumbed through the alphabetized packages, half-humming, half-muttering to himself. "Ah, here we are. Merry Hanson of SummerHill Lane." He handed the package to me and proceeded to ring up the amount.

Anxiously, I tore open the package and carefully slid out the five-by-seven color glossies. I held up the first photo—a picture of a tall, stand-up antique radio.

"These aren't my pictures." I looked at the next and the next. "None of these photos are mine." My voice quivered.

The old man lowered his spectacles and peered over the top of them. "What did you say?"

I held up the prints, showing him. "These aren't my pictures. I didn't take pictures of antique furniture."

A frown furrowed his brow. "Well, let's have a look." He checked the film size and the special instruction section on the package. Bewildered, he glanced up at me. "Must be some sort of mix-up."

No kidding, I thought.

I inhaled deeply. "How could this possibly happen?"

He shrugged. "I've never seen anything like this. Not here."

"What do you mean, sir?" Worry clutched my throat. "Did someone get my pictures by mistake?"

"Well, it certainly seems that way, but it was a simple oversight," he said, pausing to scratch his chin. "Let's see. You brought your film in yesterday morning. Monday, I believe."

"That's right—yesterday." I was in the process of making a mental note to boycott this photo shop forever—never, ever to darken the door again!

Someone came in the door behind me. It was Mom. "Is everything all right?" she asked cheerfully.

I explained the problem, and Mom reacted kindly to the old man. Certainly more compassionately than *I* had.

"My daughter's very talented," she was saying. "The school photography event means everything to her."

He nodded, fumbling around in his pocket for a cigar. "We'll just have to sit tight and wait it out and hope the other customer opens the package and discovers the mistake."

I cleared my throat, attempting to speak without shouting and without chewing him out—which is definitely what the wrinkled-faced guy deserved. "Sit tight?" I was losing it, plain and simple. "I can't do any such thing! I need those pictures immediately."

For a split second, I wished my dad was an attorney instead of an ER doctor. Thoughts of a lawsuit zipped around in my mind.

Mom wrapped up things politely and ushered me out of the store. I fussed and fumed all the way home, desperately trying to push thoughts of Ashley Horton and Stiggy Eastman out of my head.

TWENTY

Supper lasted longer than usual with Mom lecturing me about my horrid behavior at the photo lab. I tried to explain why the pictures were so important.

"They weren't just any shots, Mom. You should've seen the lighting that day—I mean, it was something out of a masterpiece painting. Honest."

She wasn't impressed. "Terrific or not, you mustn't ever lose your temper like that. The man was only trying to do his job and cover for the owners. You heard him."

I'd heard him all right, and the timing for a New York trip couldn't have been worse.

Dad showed up when we were half-finished with supper. He avoided my questions about the kidnapping and subsequent deprogramming of Mrs. Davis. He and Mom wanted to discuss things alone—I wasn't dense—so I excused myself and went to the family room to watch TV.

Within minutes, a news bulletin about Mrs. Davis came on. "Mom, Dad!" I called. "Come quick!"

They came in and stood watching as the reporter linked the strange repetitious writing to a commune of cult members hidden away in a remote hilly area several miles west of Lancaster.

"This is similar to the report I heard on the radio earlier," Mom mentioned.

"I wonder if Chelsea and her dad are watching," I said.

Dad nodded with an air of certainty. "They're doing more than watching. They're probably videotaping right now." That's all he would say.

I fidgeted, eyeing my parents more than the TV screen. Annoyed and frustrated, I finally got up and left the room. They weren't going to clue me in, that was one-hundred-percent-amen clear!

So . . . not only had Chelsea and I kept secrets from the world, now it seemed my parents had secrets of their own.

I phoned Chelsea in Dad's study, out of earshot. "Did you see the news report just now?" I asked when she answered.

"Did I ever! Wow, it looks like another one of your prayers was answered. You've been praying, haven't you, Mer?" I heard her sigh.

"I said I would, didn't I?"

She ignored my comment. "I can only hope Mom's okay . . . *if* they find her!"

"Me too." Then I got up the nerve, after former repeated rejections, to invite her to church this Sunday. "You'll never guess what we're studying in the high school class." I told her about the angel stories Mr. Burg had shared with us last week.

"Really? Angels?" She paused for a moment. Then—
"Sure, I'll come."

I nearly swallowed my tonsils. "Great, we'll pick you up."

Joy, oh joy! I completely forgot the mistake at the photo lab. My woes had vanished, just like my pictures.

Unfortunately, Chelsea asked about them. "Did you get your photos back?"

"Oh, that. Well . . ." And I began to fill her in, leaving out the part about feeling hostile and angry. Mom was right. My behavior had been mighty pitiful. Coming on the heels of this good news from Chelsea—that she was coming with me to church—well, I wanted to alter my attitude problem right then and there. Photo lab flub or not.

❧   ❧

The next day at high noon, Chelsea, Lissa, and I showed up at the sandwich shop. We sat in the booth right behind Ashley Horton and Stiggy Eastman. They didn't seem to mind, probably because we pretended not to be interested.

Chelsea hammed it up a bit much, though, calling it a coincidence that all of us had shown up for lunch at the same place. "Who would've thought!" She laughed to herself as she scooted past their table.

Later, when the right moment presented itself, Lissa got up and went to the ladies' room. Chelsea and I talked about everything under the sun, except the latest report about the commune. I kept my promise to Mom and didn't say a word about her dad's plans to kidnap-rescue her mother.

On the way back from the rest room, Lissa just happened to saunter up to Stiggy's side of the table, where he was showing off his art portfolio. "Wow," she said, staring at the picture. "Is this a winning photograph or what?"

It was our cue to get out of our seats and rush over. And we did. All three of us girls leaned over the award-winning picture, gawking.

The photo was a city scene—the square in downtown Lancaster. The street glistened with a covering of rain.

I looked more closely. Brightly colored umbrellas, Central Market in the background, and people scurrying by—the whole offering lent itself to award status. The subtle play of lighting on the pavement made for a delightful picture.

"Did you take the shot right after sunup?" I asked.

"Excellent perception," Stiggy replied. "You must be an artist, too."

"Man, is she ever," Lissa piped up, even though I tried to get her to hush. "You should see her gallery of pictures."

"Right," I said.

"Oh, Merry, don't be so modest," Chelsea said. "You're so good my grandmother wants to pay you to take pictures of her for her Christmas card this year." She turned to Stiggy. "Trust me, Merry's good!"

I smiled. "Thanks, but this guy's photography is truly amazing." I turned the group's attention back to Stiggy's work.

He seemed flattered by our oohing and ahhing, and Ashley really didn't know what to make of it. She never said a word to distract us, but I wondered if she wasn't feeling a bit ticked off and just not showing it.

Finally, she got around to introducing all of us to Stiggy. He forced a half-smile and soaked in the recognition while twiddling his thumbs. He sat tall in the booth, shifting his dark brown eyes from one girl to another. It seemed as though he'd never had to deal with accolades before. Reluctantly, we headed back to our table to finish lunch.

❧   ❧

It wasn't until Friday after school that I began to freak out over Ashley. She followed me as I headed for the school bus. "What's *your* subject matter going to be?" And before I could reply, she added, "Surely you've decided by now."

I didn't tell her my subject matter had been swallowed up at the photo lab down the street. And still no word from the old man running the place. Not even a phone call to apologize!

TWENTY-ONE

I griped to Dad at supper. "How on earth could something like this happen? You'd think after all this time someone would be wondering where his pictures are and want to trade the wrong ones for his own."

Dad nodded rather apathetically between bites.

With my fork, I poked at the carrots on my plate. "The photos of ancient furniture were probably taken by some antique dealer. I wonder if I should call around to all the dealers in town and see if they've lost some pictures."

Mom zeroed in on the word *antique*. It defined her main interest in life. "It does seem strange that someone would take pictures of antique furniture unless they were recording them for an inventory of some kind," she suggested.

"But why the enlargements—full-color glossies?" I asked, noting that Mom seemed as perplexed as I.

Dad offered no help, and I was really beginning to wonder about his preoccupied state. Was the Davis kidnapping attempt coming up? Maybe this weekend?

Mom had little to say on the Davis subject when I

pumped her for answers as we cleared the kitchen table. Both my parents were keeping a tight lid on things. "I wish you'd never told me anything about rescuing Mrs. Davis," I finally blurted out in sheer frustration.

"I only told you about it so you would pray" came the terse reply. There was no messing with Mom.

Tired of inquiring, I dropped the subject. When the kitchen was cleaned to Mom's satisfaction, I went upstairs and pulled out Levi Zook's letter. I reread it straight through, then found some floral stationery and began to write.

An hour later, Ashley Horton called.

"Merry, hi," she said. "I hope I'm not calling you at a bad time."

Now what? I wondered.

"This is fine," I said.

"Well, I'm beginning to wonder if I should even bother to enter the photo contest," Ashley whined.

"Really?"

"Oh, I don't know, I guess I'm getting cold feet after hearing how astounding Stiggy's entry is supposed to be this year."

"*This* year's photo?"

"Uh-huh."

"Have you seen it?" I asked.

"Well, no."

"Then how can you possibly know if it's any good?" She was silent.

"I sure haven't heard anything wonderful about his latest entry—except from you. Maybe Stiggy's trying to scare off his competition."

"Why would he want to do that?" she asked.

"Who knows? Maybe his picture isn't really all that great, and he's just saying it is."

"Oh, Merry," she gushed, "I wish I'd called you earlier about this. I've worried too much."

I sighed. "Just do your best. That's all any of us can do."

"That's what Jonathan keeps telling me."

My heart flipped hearing his name. "Well, he's right, you know."

She sighed into the phone. "I think he must be right about everything."

I thought I'd die or drop the phone. Or both. She was talking about *my* Jon. Again!

"Merry? You still there?"

"I'm here." I wished I weren't!

"What do you think of Jonathan Klein?"

Who was she kidding? I thought, beginning to cave in. I wondered if steam was spouting out my ears yet.

"I've known Jon for a very long time," I found myself bragging. "He and I go way back."

"Oh, really? How far?"

I wanted so badly to start alliterating to see if she could do it, too. Wanted to show her up, but I gripped the phone with my left hand and pulled on my shirt with my right.

"Why don't you ask Jon?" I blurted.

"About you and him?"

"Sure, if you want."

"Okay," she sounded a bit reluctant. "He's coming over in a few minutes."

Now I felt really foolish. What if she asked him about me like I was fishing to find out how he felt? That secondhand girl-asks-boy stuff went on all the time—but it certainly wasn't what I'd had in mind!

"Jon's going to help me with my photo shoot," she explained. "In fact, that might be him at the door now. I'd better get going. Well, 'bye, Merry. See you Sunday."

My heart was pounding ninety miles an hour as I hung up. This girl was driving me bazookas!

It was a good thing I'd nearly finished writing Levi's letter *before* Ashley called. My mind was so clogged up with the phone conversation that I simply put the letter away. I did remember, however, to cut out one of my wallet-sized school pictures and slip it into the envelope.

Standing at the window, I surveyed the cornfield across SummerHill Lane. I recounted Ashley's words and decided that she'd actually called me to flaunt Jon. He was going to her house—that's why she'd called. All that baloney about Stiggy and his wonderful work . . . it had nothing to do with anything.

I ran downstairs and grabbed a windbreaker from the hall closet. "I'm going for a walk, Mom," I called.

"Don't be long. It's getting dark."

"I know." But I wanted it to be dark. I wanted the night to close in around me. I'd been through all this before—only with Lissa Vyner last spring. Why was it that right when Jon and I were really clicking, someone else had to step in and spoil things?

TWENTY-TWO

Quickening my pace, I headed for the steep grade that led to Chelsea's house. The dusk chirped and buzzed as tiny insects and other small animals prepared for night.

Several cars were parked in the driveway at the Davis residence when I arrived. One of them was a squad car. Probably Officer Vyner's.

Chelsea came to the door carrying a golden-haired puppy. "Oh, Mer," she cooed, hugging me with her free arm, "look what Rachel Zook brought over."

I touched the cocker spaniel's neck gently. "For keeps?"

"He's all mine." Chelsea's eyes were shining as she led me upstairs to her room. "I'm going to call him Secrets."

"When did Rachel come?" I asked, settling down on her window seat.

"A little while ago." Her eyes searched mine. "Somehow or other, she heard about my mom. You never told her, did you?"

"No, but one of their Mennonite cousins may have heard about it on the news. Or—" I stopped, thinking who the true informer might've been—"maybe it was

Levi!" My smile gave me away.

Chelsea noticed. "Good old Levi. You've always liked him, haven't you?"

"We're friends, but that's all there is to it. He's off in Virginia at a Mennonite college."

She grinned, holding the puppy up for me to see. "Isn't he adorable?"

I noted the slight wave in his silky coat. Rachel had chosen Chelsea for the caretaker of her favorite pup. "Better not bring him around my cats," I warned. "They'd scratch his pretty little nose right off."

We joked about our taste in pets, then got to discussing church and what she could expect on Sunday morning. She was especially interested in the discussion on angels. "Are you sure they'll be talking more about it?" she asked, her eyes bright with anticipation.

"Positive," I said. "And since you're interested, I have to tell you something. You know the day we first went snooping in the woods?"

She nodded.

"Well, the strangest thing happened. This Bible verse I learned when I was a kid popped into my head out of nowhere. It was so unusual."

"Really? What was the verse?"

I was hoping she'd ask. "It goes like this: 'For he will command his angels concerning you to guard you in all your ways; they will lift you up in their hands, so that you will not strike your foot against a stone.' "

"That's in the Bible?" she said, eyebrows at attention.

"Sure is."

"Where?" She stood up as though she were going to get one and bring it to me.

"Do you have a Bible in the house?" I asked, surprised at this turn of events.

"Daddy does," she admitted. "It's a family book. We never read it, though."

"Well, go get it, and I'll show you the verse." This was truly incredible!

"Here, take care of Secrets." She handed the pup to me.

I caressed his tiny head and back as I often did my cats. Then in a moment, Chelsea was back, lugging the heavy book. *Thunk*, she put it to rest on the window seat.

"There. Bet you never thought you'd see the day," she announced, grinning.

I was careful not to say anything to distract from the moment. Gently, I opened the enormous Bible, locating the passage in Psalm 91.

She knelt down and read verses eleven and twelve out loud. "Hey, what a cool thing," she said. "It looks to me like the angels from heaven take their orders from . . . from God." She'd never mentioned the heavenly Father that way. My heart leaped.

There was a catch in her voice as she read the verse again out loud. Looking up, she whispered, "Can you believe it, Mer—a God who sends angels, His very own angels, to guard us on earth?"

I smiled through tears, and poor little Secrets caught a few drops on his nose. It was best that I didn't say a word. Chelsea was the one who needed to talk—to express her true inner feelings.

The sound of tires on the dirt lane caught our attention. Reluctantly, I turned to look out the window and was surprised to see my father pull up in the driveway. "What's my dad doing here?" I asked.

Chelsea peered out into the darkness. "Half the community is over here."

I didn't say anything, but I wondered about it. Rescue by kidnapping—it seemed so drastic. But love sometimes demands extreme measures.

Chelsea sat down opposite me on the window seat. "I'm glad you're my friend, Merry," she said. "I've given you a hard time about God and the Bible—all these years."

I shrugged, playing it down. "We're still friends, though, right?"

"But I think things are going to be different. I won't put you down about God anymore. I promise."

Chelsea's change of heart was a major breakthrough. One I'd been praying for. Levi and Lissa had been praying for her, too, since last spring.

She got up and switched on her matching dresser lamps. The room was filled with brilliant light, and after having sat there in the fading light of dusk, my eyes had to grow accustomed to it. I knew it would be the same for Chelsea. Just because she'd begun to recognize God as a living spirit didn't mean she was necessarily ready to accept the good news of Jesus. It would take some getting accustomed to. And Sunday was another day.

Chelsea told me to stay put. She went downstairs and soon returned carrying two cans of soda. "You know, I heard something today at school."

"What?"

"Some kid told me that Stiggy Eastman has photographed an amazing shot for this year's contest."

I snickered. "I heard it, too. From Ashley."

Chelsea stared at me. "Hey, you never told me how your photos came out."

"Well, when Mom and I went into town to pick them up, I found someone else's pictures in my package."

"Oh, Merry . . . no. What'll you do?"

"What *can* I do?" I sighed, twisting my hair. I hated discussing this topic. "If you wanna know the truth, I think the photo lab flat-out lost them."

"That's despicable."

"Maybe I'm just not supposed to enter the contest this year."

"How can you say that?"

"Look, nothing can be done except a lot of praying," I admitted.

"Well, then you better keep praying," she said, surprising me.

Something was truly changing in her. She'd never, ever said such a thing to me. Never!

"In my opinion," she said, "the old hut was the perfect choice, even though I was a little ticked at you for snapping pictures when I was so freaked."

"I know, and I'm sorry." I looked at her beautiful bedroom with its white French-provincial furniture and thick throw rugs. "I don't think I ever apologized for turning my back on you in the woods when you were so frightened."

"It's okay—no big deal. Besides, we oughta look on

the bright side. I think my mom's coming home."

"When . . . how?"

She beamed, her eyes dancing. "That's why all those people are downstairs," she informed me. "Daddy's got a plan, and I know you won't believe this, but it's true. He's going to kidnap my mom because he loves her."

I nodded, reaching for her hand. "I heard about it, I just didn't know when it would be."

She shook her head. "Mom's gonna be so bummed out over it—I can just imagine," she went on. "But in time, when everything's behind her, she'll be coming home."

We talked for a while longer, and she explained that her dad didn't want her involved in the kidnap planning. "That's why I'm glad you came over. With all the talk going on downstairs . . . well, I'm just glad you're here, Mer."

I glanced at my watch. "I better call my mom. She'll worry if I don't let her know where I am."

"Good idea," she said. "Maybe if all of us did that— let people know just exactly where we are—the world would be a better place."

I must admit, I wasn't totally sure what Chelsea was referring to, but I had a sneaking suspicion it had something to do with her new view of life and love. And God.

TWENTY-THREE

Sunday was a glorious autumn day in more ways than one. Chelsea went to Sunday school and church with us and actually raised her hand to ask questions in class.

It was strange dealing with my emotions, however. On one side of me sat exuberant Chelsea, so eager to be here, and on the opposite side was flirtatious Ashley, trying her best to get Jon's attention.

I didn't want a single thing to spoil my day with Chelsea, so I honed my concentration skills and did my best to block out all distractions.

In the hallway after class, Ashley cornered me and shared the events of her Friday evening with Jon and their cozy photo session. She reviewed every detail for my benefit.

"Sounds like things went well," I said, refusing to show a smidgen of jealousy and keeping an eye on Chelsea, who'd gone back into the classroom to talk to Mr. Burg.

"Oh, did they ever!" Ashley carried on.

"Well, if I were you, I'd steer clear of that photo lab near the school."

Her eyes burst open. "Really? That's the place Stiggy recommended to me. He said he's always gone there."

"Well, do what you want," I said, going to find Chelsea. "But don't say I didn't warn you."

Ashley cocked her head suspiciously. "Did something happen?"

I wasn't going to tell her my photographs were missing. Not in a million-trazillion years!

"Excuse me," I said, flouncing off to get Chelsea.

Mr. Burg was showing her a Scripture, and she asked to write it down. Tickled at her genuine interest, I waited patiently.

It was after the morning worship service, when people were milling around, that I ran into Jon. Actually, he ran into me. Not literally, but he was there in the lobby, smiling his wonderful grin.

I included Chelsea in our conversation, never regretting for one minute that Jon and I wouldn't be speaking alliteration-eze this time around. There were more important things in life than silly word games.

"Everyone's talking about the photography contest," Jon said with a quizzical expression on his handsome face.

I didn't volunteer any information about my lost photos, and I knew I could trust Chelsea not to mention anything either.

Jon started to alliterate a couple of times, probably out of habit. Chelsea brought up the angel discussion from Sunday school, and Jon listened, apparently pleased to see Chelsea taking interest in such things.

Monday morning, Mr. Eastman missed his daily date with the intercom. Mrs. Fields, my homeroom teacher, explained that our principal had seemed mighty upset about a roll of film. "Evidently, some prized pictures he took have become misplaced," she said before the opening announcements.

Had Mr. Eastman taken his film to the same photo lab as I had? I decided to stop by his office later—maybe during lunch.

The school secretary ended up doing his beloved duty. "Good morning, students," her sweet voice rang through the classrooms—a delightful change. "Today is Monday, October fourteenth. We will have schedule A. Faculty and students, please make a note of this."

Next came the national anthem. I leaped out of my seat, the first student standing as the warbled tape began to play. I felt truly terrific.

The past eleven days had brought traumatic ups-and-downs for all of us on SummerHill Lane. But the worst was behind us. Mr. Davis, with the help of my dad and several other men, was able to snatch Chelsea's mom away from the cult group after her evening workout at a fitness center. From what Dad says, Chelsea was right— her mom did resist the "rescue." The good news is that Berta Jean Davis will be coming home someday. Not soon, but someday.

Levi Zook? He'll be getting a letter with my picture enclosed sometime this week. I mailed it off this morning before catching the school bus. I'm glad he's listening to God's call. Still, things are going to be very different on SummerHill with Levi off at college—and overseas, too.

As for Jon Klein, he's starting to wake up and realize I'm a girl, not just a buddy—at least I think so. We don't have many classes together this semester, but today he wandered over and sat with Chelsea, Lissa, and me during lunch. Ashley scrutinized the situation from three tables away. If I had my wish, she'd back off entirely. We'll see. . . .

Miracle of miracles! My photographs were finally located. It seems that the owner's wife took them with her to New York by pure accident. And Mr. Eastman found his, too. They were the photos of antique furnishings—some that had been in his family for several generations.

Meanwhile, I guess it doesn't matter much who wins first prize in the photography contest this year. I suppose it would if that's all a girl had to look forward to. But things like hoping to lead a friend to Jesus, writing and receiving letters from a young, handsome missionary-to-be, and oh yes . . . working to improve a sagging relationship with a big brother, now those are higher goals.

The photos of the hut *are* truly incredible, however. Not because of any genius photography on my part. Serene—almost heavenly—are probably the best words to describe the one I'm going to submit for the contest. It's uncanny the way an ethereal white mist showers down over the dark house of secrets.

When I showed it to Chelsea, she got all charged up about it. "I'm telling you, Mer," she declared, "if you stare just right at the shaft of light, you'd think there was a tall, very feminine-looking angel hovering over the place."

"A what?" I studied the photo.

"Right there. See that?" She pointed, tracing the outline. "Check out that long, flowing gown. And there . . . I see wings. I do!"

"But it doesn't make sense," I argued. "Why would God's messenger be *there*?"

"Merry," she said, looking at me as if thoroughly aghast. "You prayed, don't you remember?"

I nodded, a smile bursting across my face.

Chelsea was right. I'd asked God to send His angels to watch over us. Maybe there *was* an angel in the photo, but maybe there wasn't. Someday in heaven, I would know for sure.

I thought of my twin sister. "Hey, Faithie already knows," I said, perched on Chelsea's window seat, facing out toward the dusk.

Chelsea sat cross-legged next to me. We gazed at the first star of the evening. Its light crowded out the navy blue darkness, topping off our day. "Are you sure she knows?" she asked softly.

I leaned back against the wall and smiled at my friend. "One-hundred-percent-amen sure."